With a sigh, Snake said, "Lord Digby was always eager to further Your Majesty's interests. Before he left on his inspection of forests, he asked me if there was anything he might do to assist the Old Blades. I did mention one place he might look at if he was in the vicinity—"

"Oh, you did?" the King raged. "And what was the place he was to scout for you?"

"The name escapes me for the moment," Snake said crossly, and did not flinch under his liege lord's disbelieving scowl. "I shall put my best man to work on it right away."

"Meaning who?" The King rarely bothered with details. Anger was making him meddlesome.

This time Snake balked openly. "I prefer not to mention the name here, sire. But Your Majesty will know who I mean when I refer to 'the King's Daggers.'"

"Stalwart?" roared the King, making Snake wince. "He's only a child!"

"With respect, Your Grace, for this job he is the best man you have."

Other Books by
Dave Duncan

Sir Stalwart:
Book One of the King's Daggers

THE KING'S BLADES TRILOGY
The Gilded Chain
Lord of the Fire Lands
Sky of Swords

THE CROOKED HOUSE

Book Two of the King's Daggers

DAVE DUNCAN

AVON BOOKS
An Imprint of HarperCollins*Publishers*

 For information address HarperCollins Children's Books, a division of HarperCollins Publishers, 1350 Avenue of the Americas, New York, NY 10019.

Library of Congress Catalog Card Number: 99-69745
ISBN: 0-380-80099-3

First Avon Books edition, 2000

❖

There was a crooked man,
  Who walked a crooked mile.
He found a crooked sixpence
  Against a crooked stile.

He bought a crooked cat
  Which caught a crooked mouse;
And they all lived together
  In a little crooked house.

—TRADITIONAL

Contents

Prologue: The Monster War 1

1: Murder in the Court 3

2: His Majesty's Displeasure 8

3: Posthaste 19

4: Prime 32

5: Return of the Lost Lamb 46

6: Pilot on Board 62

7: Nythia 69

8: The Sheriff of Waterby 84

9: Stalwart Sends a Message 92

10: Mervyn 97

11: The House of Smealey 103

12: The Hole 112

13: Homecoming 124

14: Reunion 133
15: Unwelcome Discovery 144
16: Meanwhile, His Sword 148
17: Baron Smealey 152
18: Sir Emerald 163
19: The Seventh Brother 170
20: A Sleight Problem 185
21: Faces from the Past 189
22: Point of View 197
23: Change of Heart 201
24: Stalwart Stalwart 209
25: Secret Passage 222
26: The Fall of the House of Smealey 230

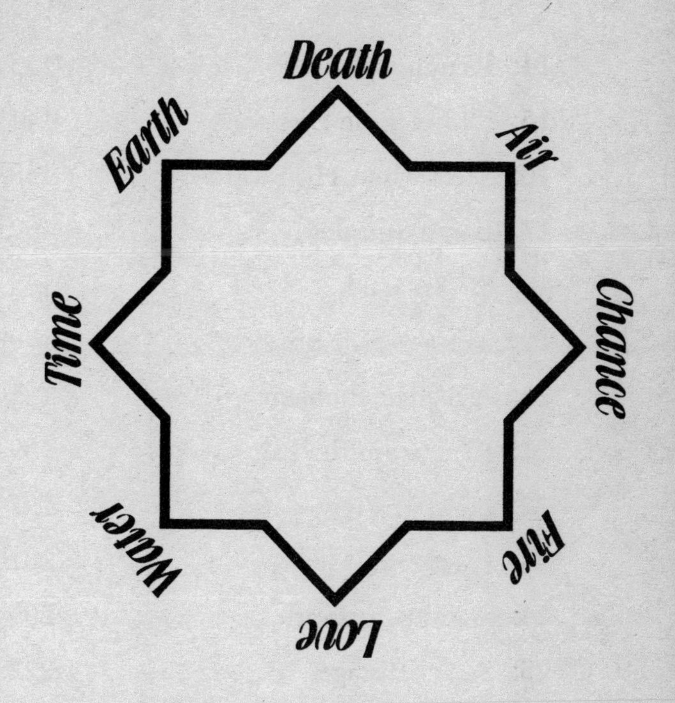
Death
Air
Chance
Fire
Love
Water
Time
Earth

Prologue: The Monster War

When King Ambrose of Chivial decided to banish black magic and stop the sale of curses and other such evils, some sorcerers retaliated by trying to kill him. Giant dogs came climbing in his windows; half-human catlike things ambushed him in the forest. Fortunately, he was well protected by the finest swordsmen in the world, the Blades of the Royal Guard, and also by the White Sisters, who were known as "sniffers" because they had the ability to detect magic. While the Guard and the Sisters defended the King, Sir Snake and a group of other daredevils, former guardsmen, attempted to track down the traitors.

By the summer of 368, the Guard was desperate for more Blades to replace those who had been slain in the war. The swordsman school of Ironhall was running boys through their training faster than ever and still could not keep up with the demand.

The book *Sir Stalwart* told how King Ambrose went there in Eighthmoon and recruited the four most senior candidates, binding them to absolute loyalty in the ancient magical ritual that included a sword stroke through the heart. The next most senior boy, Stalwart, was the best fencer in the school at the time, but everyone agreed he looked far too young to be dressed up as a guardsman. Instead of being bound, therefore, he was secretly enlisted in the Guard and assigned to help Snake. The youngest Blade of all became one of the "Old Blades," but to avoid alerting the traitors' spies, a story was spread that he had run away from Ironhall.

Wart and Sister Emerald, most junior of the White Sisters, uncovered a nest of sorcerers at a place called Quagmarsh. King Ambrose was so impressed by their success that he began referring to the pair of them as, *"the King's Daggers."*

1 Murder in the Court

It began with a murder. Stalwart saw it happen. He was watching a formal court reception, a grand state function held only three or four times a year. That was the last place anyone would expect to see such a gruesome crime.

The day's pomp had been staged in honor of the new ambassador from Isilond. King Ambrose had set out to impress him with spectacle and splendor, sparing no expense—drum rolls and trumpeters and heralds wearing gaudy tabards. Every ambassador in the diplomatic corps was there, as were scores of great lords and ladies, bejeweled and decked out in finery. They had all been escorted in from the gates of Nocare Palace by glittering honor guards of the Household Yeomen in silver-bright breastplates and plumed helmets. At the doors of the reception hall they had observed White Sisters in their snowy robes and high pointed hats—no one would sneak any evil magic into the King's presence while the Sisters were on duty. The inside of the hall was patrolled by Blades of the Royal Guard, the world's finest swordsmen.

And yet a murder!

After welcoming the new ambassador, the King began handing out honors and appointments. The first man the heralds called forward was Sir Snake. In recognition of his triumph over the traitors at Quagmarsh, he was being promoted from member to officer in the Order of the White Star, the greatest order of chivalry in the realm. It was an honor very few Blades had ever achieved. As he knelt to receive the diamond-studded brooch from the King, the assembled courtiers clapped and cheered.

Hidden away by himself on a screened balcony, Stalwart kept his hands in his armpits. *He* should have been down there as well, and he had let Snake talk him out of it. It was *he* who had made Snake's triumph at Quagmarsh possible! The King had been so impressed by that exploit that he had appointed Stalwart to the White Star, although he was *at least* ten years younger than anyone else who had ever been so honored. And stupid Stalwart had let Snake talk him out of public recognition for the time being. His undercover work for the Old Blades was too important to give up so soon, Snake had insisted, so why not just accept the star this evening during a private supper with the King? He could watch from this private box, seeing without being seen, hidden away like a shameful secret.

He had seen the King often enough at Ironhall, although never wearing his crown and swathed in a robe so massive that it needed four pages to carry its train. Ambrose was a huge man, towering over everyone else as he stood in front of his throne. At his back, with swords drawn, stood the newest Blades, who only two weeks ago had been Stalwart's classmates at Ironhall: Sir Rufus, Sir Orvil, Sir Panther, and Sir Dragon. They looked very smart in their blue and silver livery. He kept imagining the expressions on their faces if they heard his name proclaimed and saw him strutting forward before the entire court, honored as no man of his age had ever been honored.

Sigh!

And tomorrow he would ride off to a paltry little town called Horselea to investigate rumors of black magic there. In spite of all Snake's efforts to make it seem dangerous and exciting, this sounded like a very dull mission, not the sort of thing to challenge an eager young swordsman. He could not help wondering if Snake just did not know what to do with his young helper now and was sending him off to horrible Horselea to age a few years.

Sigh again!

The reception that should have been the greatest moment of his life proceeded without him, dribbling down in boredom through awards, titles, and appointments to mere acknowledgments. Peers presented stripling sons and new wives to the King. Very subtly, people were fidgeting. Even Ambrose seemed to be hurrying things along, as if hungry for the roast boar, stuffed peacock, and other delights of the state banquet that was to follow.

The herald was close to the end of the list now. In a voice like a trumpet he proclaimed, "Lord Digby of Chase, Warden of the King's Forests, knight in the Loyal and Ancient Order of the King's Blades, most humbly craves Your Majesty's gracious leave to return to court."

Digby had visited Ironhall a year or two back, and thus was one of the very few people in the hall, other than Blades, whom Stalwart recognized. He began his advance to the steps of the throne. His petition was a mere formality, because he was one of the King's personal friends. Having just returned from a brief absence, he was required by protocol to pay his respects to His Majesty at a public function. In fact he had supped with the King the previous evening and reported on his travels at that time. So it should have all been over in a few seconds. He made the first of the three low bows required. He took two more steps.

He dropped dead.

All the White Sisters standing around the hall screamed in unison. Heralds rushed forward to help the stricken man. One of them leaped up in horror with blood on his hands. Lord Digby had been stabbed through the heart. There had been no one near him; there was no weapon in sight.

It was only a wild guess, but Stalwart was instantly certain that he would not be riding to Horselea after all. He was going to be needed.

2

His Majesty's Displeasure

King Ambrose of Chivial was not merely very large, he was often very loud as well. Royally enraged by the murder of his friend, he canceled the banquet, sent the distinguished guests away, and summoned the Privy Council. Its members needed time to assemble, and he was not accustomed to waiting for anyone. He strode up and down his council chamber, roaring like a thunderstorm, while those councillors who had been foolish enough to be prompt stood back against the walls, staying out of his way.

Kings have few real friends, so Ambrose's grief was genuine. He raved that he had been grossly insulted in his own throne room and Chivial would be the laughingstock of all Eurania. Although he would never admit it, he had received a severe shock, because obviously the evil sorcery had really been directed at him. Digby had died by mistake.

"Disgraced! Shamed! Sorcery most foul!" Like a gigantic bluebottle circling a kitchen, the King came to a sudden and unheralded halt. He was in front of Commander Bandit, who stood at his post in front of the door. "Why did the Guard not prevent this outrage?"

Swordsmen must be nimble, so no Blade was ever very large; Sir Bandit had to bend his head back to meet the royal glare. He said calmly, "If Your Majesty believes that the Guard is at fault, then I humbly beg leave to surrender my commission to Your Majesty."

The King seemed to swell even more. His already inflamed face turned a deeper shade of purple. "You are responsible for our safety!"

Bandit was popular with his guardsmen because he never lost his temper. Nor would he allow them to be unfairly blamed. "With all respect, sire, your Blades cannot defend you against sorcery unless it is identified for them. That responsibility rests with the Sisters."

Ambrose flashed a look around the room to confirm what he already knew. "And where is Mother Superior?"

"Her Excellency was absent from court, Your Grace, and had only just returned to the palace when she was informed of the incident and Your Majesty's summons. I believe she wished to ascertain—"

A tap on the door made even the imperturbable Bandit look relieved. "With Your Grace's permission . . ."

The King moved just enough to let him peer out and then admit the lady in question. Mother Superior was a national monument, who had been around court longer than anyone could remember—tall, imperious, unsmiling, and relentlessly efficient. Her white robes were invariably spotless and uncreased, and the high hennin that all White Sisters wore seemed to brush the lintel of the tall doorway. Finding herself trapped between the paneled wall and the King's angry glare, she dropped without hesitation into a curtsey that almost poked that white conical hat right in his piggy little eyes. Ambrose perforce backed up.

"Well, Mother?" he bellowed. "Who brought such sorcery into the hall? Why did your women not give warning? They were guarding the doors. What do I pay you for, if not protection, eh? Explain your failure!"

Rising, she inspected his rage with matronly disapproval, as if it were a child's tantrum. "The Sisters failed to give warning because the sorcery was *not* brought into the hall, sire."

"A courtier is struck down on the steps of the

throne by an invisible assassin and you claim there was no sorcery present?"

She raised her chin. "With respect, sire, there was no *invisible assassin.* I have spoken with the Prioress and most of the Sisters who were present. They are adamant that there was no sorcery present until the instant Lord Digby died."

"How can that be? What sort of magic works like that?"

She met the royal glare with one of her own. "I do not know what sort of magic, sire! None of the Sisters has ever met anything quite like it. They detected no death elementals. Air and fire, they think. And love! A large measure of love."

"Love?" roared the King. "A spell drops a man dead and you say it is made of *love*?"

Even the formidable Mother Superior flinched before that enormous bellow. "So they claim."

"And it kills when it is not there? Instantaneously? From a distance? *What sort of magic does that?"*

"The Sisters can only determine the presence of elemental spirits, Your Majesty, not analyze the compulsions laid on them. That is the job of the College."

With a snarl of fury, King Ambrose swung around to survey the assembled councillors. The

Lord High Admiral was there, the Lord Chamberlain, several dukes, the Earl Marshal . . . but not the head of the Royal College of Conjury. Inevitably, the royal eye sought out the crimson robes and gold chain of Lord Chancellor Roland. "Where is Grand Wizard, Chancellor? He was at the investiture."

As Sir Durendal, Lord Roland had been the most famous Blade of them all, commander of the Guard before Bandit. He bowed calmly. "Sire, the learned adept is deeply concerned about Your Grace's safety in the face of this unprecedented threat. He wished to consult urgently with the entire faculty, so I gave him leave—" He was cut off by a royal bellow. Everyone knew that Grand Wizard was a mild-tempered scholar who became flustered when the King shouted at him, whereas Lord Roland accepted that his duties sometimes included acting as royal punching bag. Like now, for instance.

"Bah! He dared not face us, you mean! Does he have the faintest idea how that evil was worked?"

"I suspect not, Your Grace. But the sooner he can set the College to work the better."

"Snake!" The royal anger turned on Lord Roland's companion. As thin as his namesake,

Snake was dandily dressed in a green velvet jerkin, cloth-of-gold britches, silk hose, fur-trimmed robe, and osprey-plumed hat. He made a leg with a fencer's fluid grace. "Sire?"

"That!" The King poked a meaty finger at him.

Snake looked down. "Oh, that."

"Yes! *That!*" Ambrose had dropped his voice to a low growl. He was much more dangerous when he was quiet than when he was shouting. The *that* in question was the glittering six-pointed star he had hung around Snake's neck not two hours ago. "I gave you that because you told me you had wiped out the traitor sorcerers who keep trying to kill me. It would seem that you lied."

Snake would never have made such a claim, but he did not deny the accusation. He just quirked his eyebrows as if puzzled. His features were narrow and bony, like the rest of him; he had an extraordinarily arrogant nose and a thin, disdainful mustache. "It would seem we missed a few, sire."

"And what are you doing about them now?"

"I consulted with Grand Wizard as he was leaving, and he agreed that action at a distance like that is a highly original, if not unique, application of magic. He is also of the opinion, Your

Grace, that the range of such an enchantment must be limited, and therefore the spell must have been cast from somewhere very close to the palace—probably within Grandon itself or its suburbs."

Everyone knew that Ambrose detested being lectured, but Snake blithely continued and was not struck down by any royal thunderclaps. The King listened, scowling intently.

"Of course Your Majesty is aware that powerful spells tend to leave traces on the octogram where they were cast, at least for a short while. I therefore suggested to Mother Superior that the Sisters who were present in the hall at the time of the crime, and who should therefore be able to recognize the, er, *smell* of the murderous enchantment, be sent to inspect every known octogram within an hour's coach ride of the palace. Fortunately, we had already compiled such a list, so this program is now under way. I sent Old Blades along to defend the good ladies. A dozen carriages are even now making the rounds, and they will visit every elementary in or near the capital."

That was incredibly fast work, and could not be faulted.

"Bah! Anyone can make an octogram with a piece of chalk and a reasonably clean floor."

Snake bowed again. "Your Majesty's expertise is legendary."

The King's glare turned even darker. "So why would the traitors not have created a new octogram, one you don't know about?"

"Of course they may have done so, sire. However, Grand Wizard did point out that great time and effort are required to season a new octogram before it will work predictably. He suggested we begin by inspecting the known sites."

"Harumph! But you have no idea who was behind this foul attempt on our life?"

Snake pursed his lips, as if he had somehow tugged the ends of that arrogant mustache. "Has Your Majesty considered the possibility that the attack was directed at the man it slew?"

The King's mouth opened and shut a few times. His eyes seemed to shrink even smaller, retreating into their nests of blubber.

"I may be quite wrong, of course." Snake obviously did not believe that. "But this is a new and very horrible sort of conjuration. Would the evil genius who could devise such a weapon be so clumsy as to mistake Digby for Your Grace?"

"Why," Ambrose growled, even quieter, "would he be so perverse as to want to kill our Warden of Forests?" Only loyalty to his late friend would keep him from pointing out that Digby had been an amiable blockhead—a fine sportsman, but of no real importance.

Snake glanced around as if to see who was listening. Predictably, the entire Privy Council was hanging on every word. "Possibly because he knew something, sire? Something dangerous to the traitors?"

"Harumph! He spent the last month counting stags and partridges all over the realm. What could possibly be dangerous about that information?"

"Er, nothing, sire. . . . He mentioned nothing untoward last night?"

Monarchs were not accustomed to being questioned, and Snake's presumption did not soothe the royal temper. The only answer was a head shake and a dangerous glare.

"It is unfortunate, sire, that I just returned to court myself last night and had no chance to speak with the late lord."

"Indeed?" the King said with menace. "And what exactly would *you* have had to discuss with Lord Digby?"

Again Snake glanced around the room, then peered up hopefully at the King. "May I answer that question in private audience, sire?"

"You believe there are *spies* in our Privy Council?"

"Of course not, sire." But the traitors must have eyes and ears at court. Rumors spread faster than bad smells. The palace swarmed with servants, all of whom knew enough to keep their ears open for any good scrap of news or gossip, and where to take it to turn it into gold. Ambrose knew as well as anyone that the more people who knew a secret, the greater the chance that everyone soon would.

With a sigh, Snake said, "Lord Digby was always eager to further Your Majesty's interests. Before he left on his inspection of forests, he asked me if there was anything he might do to assist the Old Blades. I did mention one place he might look at if he was in the vicinity—"

"Oh, you did?" the King raged. "We recall giving strict orders that the Old Blades were to be old Blades and nothing but old Blades, that you were to recruit no one who was not a knight in the Order."

That remark was met by an awkward pause, because of course Digby had indeed been a knight in the Loyal and Ancient Order of the King's Blades, although he had been the same age as the King himself, so his youthful days of swaggering around in livery were twenty years in the past. Then Ambrose realized his mistake. The royal roar returned, fit to rattle the windows.

"We expressly forbade Lord Digby to join the Old Blades!"

Snake did not say that he had never been told of that edict, although his eyebrows hinted it. "There was no question of joining, Your Grace, just a small and very harmless favor that he—"

"And what was the place he was to scout for you?"

"The name escapes me for the moment," Snake said crossly, and did not flinch under his liege lord's disbelieving scowl. "I shall put my best man to work on it right away."

"Meaning who?" The King rarely bothered with details. Anger was making him meddlesome.

This time Snake balked openly. "I prefer not to mention the name here, sire. But Your Majesty will know who I mean when I refer to 'the King's Daggers.'"

"Stalwart?" roared the King, making Snake wince. "He's only a child!"

"With respect, Your Grace, for this job he is the best man you have."

3 Posthaste

The storm had been building over Starkmoor for hours. It broke just before sunset, sweeping down in fury on the Blackwater valley, flaunting flames of lightning and drum rolls of thunder. It hurled apples from trees and flattened corn, as if to warn that summer was over at last. Long before it hit, though, Osbert had rounded up the horses from the meadow. By the time the rain and hail began thundering on the slates, he had them all combed and curried and comfortably bedded down in their stalls.

Obviously no travelers would be coming by on a night like this, but he could not just run for the house and take the rest of the evening off. Not yet. Thunder made horses restless. So he found a comfortable seat on a bale of straw in the covered saddling area outside the tack shed. From there he could see into most of the stalls that lined either side of the yard, and hear the remarks being whinnied back and forth. If there was any panic, he could move to stop it before it grew serious. He was contentedly munching an apple and marveling at the white haze of hail rebounding from every hard surface, when he heard an answering whinny from the lane.

In through the gate came three horses. Two of them bore bedraggled riders; the third was a well-laden sumpter. He scrambled to his feet and watched angrily as they splashed along the yard toward him.

Osbert Longberry ran the Blackwater post house as his father and grandfather had run it before him. He loved horses so dearly that he could imagine no better life. He made sure his charges ate well, even when he and his family did not. When a sickly or weary horse was brought in—one that any sensible hostler would trade out again as fast as possible—he would often keep it for weeks, until he had wormed it, pampered it, and nursed it back to health. A post-horse might be traded from house to house across the length and breadth of Chivial, but if one that had spent time at Blackwater ever came back, Osbert always remembered it.

The village lay only an hour's ride from the King's great school of Ironhall. Every few days some Blade or royal courier would go by on

Crown business. They liked to have a fresh mount for the climb up Starkmoor, which was a steep trek. Coming back down was equally hard on a horse, so they would change mounts again on the way home. Osbert approved of the Blades; Ironhall taught them almost as much about horses as about swords, and they treated their mounts with almost as much respect. They spurned the common posting animals. The King boarded a string of royal horses with Osbert Longberry and came by every few months with his Royal Guard escort. His Majesty never failed to hail Osbert by name and wish him good chance.

These new arrivals were quality stock—he could tell that just by watching their approach, although the storm was naturally making them skittish. In Osbert's opinion, any responsible rider would have taken shelter under trees or in the lee of a building until the worst of the weather had blown over—certainly until the hail ended. He would perhaps forgive a royal courier for treating a horse so, because his business might be urgent, with every hour counting. He could see that these two were mere boys, but old enough to know better.

As soon as they were safely in under cover, the visitors dismounted. One of them jumped down nimbly and removed his hat to shake off the water, revealing a very clumsily cropped head of blond stubble. The other moved more circumspectly, but he was no older or taller. He had a chubbier face and dark hair down to his shoulders. Neither of them could be a day more than fourteen. Osbert looked them over suspiciously—it was not unknown for horse thieves to visit a post house and try to exchange their loot for honest animals. These two were too well dressed for that, he decided. The blond one's fur-trimmed cloak stuck out at the back, proof that he was wearing a sword. The other appeared to be unarmed, although his clothes were equally fine. They must be just rich young gentlemen, who had never been taught proper respect for horseflesh.

"Terrible weather you keep around here," the blond kid said cheekily, wiping his face and thrusting reins at Osbert. "I need your three best right away. There'll be a silver groat for you if you're quick!"

Osbert scowled. "Can't send honest animals out in this weather, lad."

The blond boy had already set off toward the stalls to see what mounts were available. He stopped and spun around, frowning.

"I'm in a hurry."

"It won't kill you to be an hour late for dinner. Might kill a horse to catch a chill."

The rich brat smirked. "*Please? Pretty* please?"

Mockery infuriated Osbert. "No! Go and choose a horse if you like, but I won't let it out of here until the storm passes."

The two boys exchanged cryptic glances, but the dark-haired boy said nothing. The blond boy shrugged and turned.

"Not that way. Those are the King's horses." Osbert pointed to the other side of the yard. "Choose from there."

The kid drew himself up to his full height, which wasn't very much. He tried to look stern and succeeded only in seeming sulky. "We are on the King's business. We ride to Ironhall."

Spoiled brat! Osbert knew his type. All his life his father's money had let him have anything he wanted, so now he just fancied some fencing lessons, did he? Well, if he thought money would get him into Ironhall, he was sadly mistaken. They didn't take rich trash there, because rich trash wouldn't last a week under the discipline.

"Another hour won't hurt much, sonny. It takes five years to make a Blade."

The kid's face flamed scarlet. He reached under his cloak for his sword. Osbert yelped in fright and leaped backward, colliding with the sumpter.

"Wart!" shouted the other boy. "Don't!"

"Don't what?" The would-be swordsman scowled.

"He's not armed."

The blond boy's scowl turned to exasperation, as if all the world was crazy except him. "I can see that! You think I'd draw on . . . on him?" He turned to Osbert. "Know what this is?"

He was showing the hilt of his sword, and it bore a yellow jewel. Osbert had seen hundreds like it. Only Blades sported cat's-eye swords. The kid wasn't hoping to *enroll* in Ironhall. . . . Osbert gaped at him in disbelief.

"You can't be!"

The boy's eyes narrowed in fury. "Yes, I am! And whether I am of the Royal Guard or a private Blade, by law I can take any horse in your stable. Right?"

"Yes, Sir Blade."

"Any horse!"

"Yes, Your Honor!"

"I could take *all* of them!"

"Yes, yes! Beg pardon. I didn't . . . Sorry."

The boy turned his back angrily and strode off to inspect the King's horses.

The other boy was smiling apologetically.

"He's sensitive about his looks. He's older than he seems, obviously." Since he was unarmed, he must be the Blade's ward, but he was far too young to be a minister of the Crown or an ambassador. Most likely he was some obscure member of the royal family, to have been honored with such a bodyguard.

"Yes, my lord. Sorry about the misunderstanding. I did hear that the King was taking them younger than usual, because of the Monster War." But, even so . . .

"He's a very good swordsman," said the boy, "and he truly is on urgent business for the King."

"Yes, my lord." Osbert hurried off after the baby-faced Blade to help him select his horses.

By the time they were saddled and the baggage had been transferred to the new sumpter, the storm had faded to a heavy rain, so the argument had been unnecessary. Surprisingly, the Blade did give Osbert the silver groat he had promised, and he did sign for the horses: *Stalwart, companion*. Some of his brethren would not have been so forgiving.

As he rode out of the gate, he turned to the companion riding beside him. "Just so you know, I do *not* use my sword on unarmed yokels. I'd only do that if they attacked me first."

"I'm sorry. You startled me. And you scared him half to death!"

Stalwart chuckled. "He thought you were a boy!"

"Am I supposed to feel flattered?" she asked.

The hostler had not been the first to mistake Emerald for a boy that day, although Stalwart had refrained from mentioning the fact sooner. It was a natural mistake when she was dressed like a man, for she was as tall as he was (or he was as short as she was, depending on how one looked at the problem). She had fooled even him for a moment when they had met before dawn in the palace stables. Only then had he realized that she obviously could not ride a horse in a White Sister's flowing draperies, not to mention the absurd steeple hat. When he asked where she had found such garments in the middle of the night, she had become strangely vague. Who could guess what deceptions the White Sisters might get up to that no man ever heard about? Perhaps they made a habit of masquerading as men. He would ask Snake when he got back.

It had been Snake who had suggested Emerald come along. He must have learned at Valglorious that she could ride like a trooper, but Snake always knew everything. Stalwart had not cared much for the idea. After all, his new mission was merely to find out whatever it was Lord Digby had discovered earlier, the secret that had caused him to be murdered. Digby had not needed a White Sister to help him. If an old man like Digby could do it, Stalwart could. But the King had thought it was a good idea, and that had settled it.

She was doing remarkably well, although Stalwart knew better than to say so—she would bite his face off. She had not uttered one word of complaint, and she looked no more tired than he felt. Of course he was leading the packhorse, so he had to have an eye in the back of his head all the time; that made his job a little harder, but not much.

It had been a very long day. The King's little supper party had not finished until well after midnight. They had set out at first light and ridden all the way from Grandon without a break, pausing only to change horses. That was how Snake traveled. *Never give your enemies time to find out you're coming,* he said. Besides, this mission was urgent. If the traitor sorcerers had learned how to kill people at a distance, then the King might drop dead at any minute. It was up to Sir Stalwart to track down the evil in time, a *huge* responsibility!

As they left Blackwater and walked the horses up the winding hill trail, Emerald said, "You never said we were bound for Ironhall. I thought we were going to Prail, to catch the ferry."

"We are. Ironhall is only a little way off the Prail road."

"Why?" she asked suspiciously. "You just want to go back and gloat?"

"Of course not!" He mustn't, but he had been thinking wistfully about the idea all afternoon. He kept imagining himself strolling into the hall when everyone was at dinner, wandering up to the high table to sit with the knights and masters, since he was a real Blade now. He would have *Sleight,* his cat's-eye rapier, slung at his thigh and the White Star jewel glittering on his jerkin. Very few Blades had ever earned that honor, and he had done it in less than two weeks. He kept thinking of Grand Master's face when he saw it. . . . He would have to tell them about Quagmarsh. He might mention in passing how he had taken on two swordsmen at once and killed both of them. That was not a Blade record, but not something that happened every day, either. And if the conversation should happen to touch on that party last night with him and the King playing duets on their lutes . . . then he might let slip the complimentary remarks the great Durendal had made, Lord Roland, the greatest Blade of—

"Then why are we going there?" Emerald snapped.

"What? Where?"

"Ironhall!"

"Oh, for Badger."

"A horse?"

"A man. Good friend, next behind me in seniority, so he must be Prime now."

The sun had set. A streak of red sky showed through the rain, squeezed between the lowering clouds above and the bleak moor below. The school would be eating dinner, so he was too late to make the dramatic entrance, even had it been permissible. It wasn't. He must remain a coward a little longer, the secret swordsman, the *boy* who looked too young to be dangerous. However humiliating that was, his mission was too important to risk. But he *was* growing now. At last! In another few months he'd have a mustache. . . .

"Why?" Emerald persisted.

"Why what?"

"Badger."

"Oh, Badger." Badger had a beard like a farrier's rasp. "He knows where we're going. He's been there. I remember him mentioning it. We'll take him along as a guide."

"Will Grand Master let him go?"

"Of course," Stalwart said confidently. If Grand Master refused, Stalwart could overrule him. He would enjoy doing that. He did not like Grand Master. Nobody did. Even the old knights, the retired Blades who hung around Ironhall, disapproved of him. He was surly and unpredictable, known behind his back as Small Master. For Stalwart to pull out his commission with the King's seal and start giving Grand Master orders would help make up for some of the miseries old sour face had inflicted on him over the last four years.

"Why didn't you mention him sooner?"

"Didn't I?" In fact the Badger brainwave had hit him about noon. He hadn't mentioned it then because it was such a good idea that he should have thought of it much sooner.

"Suppose this Badger doesn't want to come?"

"I shall appeal to his loyalty." That was something else Snake had taught him—you never *ordered* a man into mortal danger. You asked him. In Snake's case you shamed him, outwitted him, or flattered him until he found himself volunteering, but you never ordered. Badger might refuse, because he was a moody, self-contained loner who had made few friends at Ironhall. He was older than Stalwart and would not enjoy taking his orders. On the other hand, he was going to be offered a chance to do a real service for his king, plus a chance to see the world again after being shut up on Starkmoor for four years. He would be a fool to refuse.

They had reached the top of the first slope, and the trail ran level ahead into the gloom. The rain was easing off.

"Giddyap!" Stalwart said, digging in his heels. They would reach Ironhall about curfew, and Prail around midnight. Perfect timing! Snake would approve of his progress so far.

4 Prime

Unaware of the dread destiny bearing down on him, Badger lay stretched out on his cot in the seniors' dormitory, staring at the boards of the ceiling. He was flaming mad. Had he flamed any hotter, he would have set his blanket on fire. He had very nearly punched Grand Master in the nose. He was seriously wondering if he should go back down and finish the job.

No day was good for him now, and the nights were worse, but this day had been especially irksome. Until two weeks ago, he had been comfortably anonymous, sixth man in a senior class of nine. Now he was Prime, meaning he was saddled with a million ill-defined duties, of which the worst was being den mother to the whole school.

That morning, as he'd come out of a dreary-dull lecture on court protocol, he had been accosted by a deputation of sopranos, the most junior class. They had complained shrilly that Travers was still wetting the bed every night and making their dorm stink. So Badger had taken young Travers aside for yet another heart-to-heart talk. Travers was barely thirteen and ought to be home with his mother, if he had one. He wasn't even showing much promise as a fencer. Grand Master should never have admitted him.

"Bad dreams?" Badger asked.

Travers wailed, "Monsters!" and started to weep.

Every candidate in Ironhall was having bad dreams about monsters—except, ironically, Badger himself, who had worse things to dream about.

"Are you still quite certain that you want to be a Blade?" he asked patiently. "If you made a mistake, then it's better to admit it to yourself now than five years from now. Look at Stalwart. He ran away, but only after he'd wasted four years of his life."

There was something very suspicious about that story, though. At times Wart had been a smart aleck, rambunctious, immature pest, but he had never impressed Badger as a quitter. Most people believed Grand Master had thrown him out in one of his petty temper tantrums.

"But what can I do?" Travers wailed, his eyes

wide and red as his mouth. "If I leave, I'll be sent out onto the moors by myself and I'll starve to death!" Only orphans or rejects or rebels came to Ironhall. Very few had family to go back to.

"That's hog swill. Carters bring food to Ironhall every single day, yes? If they see a boy on the road they give him a ride into Prail or Blackwater, depending which way they're going."

The kid gasped like a convicted felon receiving a royal pardon on the steps of the gallows. *"Honest?"*

"Honest. And when they get him there, they see he gets a job in the fields or the mines or on a boat. Ironhall pays them to do this, because the Blades don't want to be accused of littering the countryside with beggars." Or skeletons; Badger didn't say that. "It will be lowly labor, not glamorous like strutting around beside the King, but there won't be any monsters."

Travers gaped at him, struck dumb by the immensity of the decision required.

Badger sighed. "Why don't you think it over for a couple of days? If you do decide to go, I'll see you get a packet of food to take, and perhaps we can steal a warm cloak for you. Don't tell anyone I told you all this."

* * *

The storm struck soon after, cascading white hail off the gloomy black walls and towers, sending peals of thunder echoing through the hills. A riding class of fuzzies and beansprouts was caught out on the moors and soaked to the skin. No one was injured, but the thunder made three horses bolt. Losing control of a horse was a serious offense. Master of Horse sentenced the riders to triple stable duties for a week, which meant that all of their free time and part of their sleeping time would be spent shoveling *horse stuffing*. News of this ghastly punishment was whispered around.

The main result of the bad weather was to move fencing classes indoors, and that brought problems for everyone, including Prime. The gym was crowded, noisy, and poorly lit. Men became testy. The juniors began clowning or goofing off. People could get hurt.

Swords clattered from dawn until dusk in Ironhall. The candidates were drilled with swords every day from their admission as spindly-limbed urchins until the night they strode out into the world behind their wards, deadly Blades bound to absolute loyalty. Master of Rapiers and Master of Sabers and their assistant knights taught fundamentals to the beginners, coached the seniors in the finer points, and tried to keep track of every one of the hundred candidates' progress. They simply did not have time to conduct all the daily practice sessions, so older boys were required to drill younger. There was no escaping that chore, although every candidate in three centuries had cursed it in his time.

In this year 368 of the House of Ranulf the problem was acute. Twenty-four men of the Order had died in the Monster War so far—eight guardsmen and sixteen knights—and Commander Bandit was screaming for more Blades to defend the King and his children. Ironhall had supplied forty in less than a year, but now it had reached its limit. The normal five-year course had been cut to four. There were only six seniors, instead of about twenty, and not one of the six was completely up to standard. They knew that. Everyone knew it. Yet they also knew that their binding could not be long delayed. The Guard would soon lick their fencing into shape for them, even if they had to work at it twenty-four hours a day, but they might find themselves facing mortal peril even sooner, ready or not. The seniors were worried young men. They grudged the hours they were forced to spend coaching juniors. Tempers were growing steadily shorter.

There was no rule that said Prime was responsible for keeping order in the fencing gym, but Grand Master was nowhere to be seen, typically. The fencing masters were demonstrating basic moves to teams of juniors. Everyone else was dueling, one on one, far too many men in far too small a space, and all the coaches were yelling directions at all the students. The result was earsplitting confusion: "Violet!" "Eggbeater!" "Higher!" "No, you *never* use Cockroach against Willow!" "Lower!" "Watch that wrist!" "That was Steeple, I said Rainbow. . . ." Feet stamped up choking clouds of dust. Thunder roared outside.

Chaos. Someone was sure to get hurt.

No sooner thought than done. Marlon, who was Second, appeared with a split lip and a broken tooth. He was the best fencer in the school at the moment, but even his agility had failed to parry a wild and unpredictable stroke. Of course he should have been wearing a mask, but it was easier to instruct without one. Badger sent him off to find Master of Rituals, who would have to assemble a team of eight to chant a healing conjuration over him in the Forge, where the school octogram was located. That would take most of the afternoon and tie up masters or knights who could have helped here.

To relieve the pressure on space, Badger conscripted about thirty of the middle classes—beardless and fuzzies—and started drilling them in calisthenics, which needed a lot less room than fencing. He had no authority to do so, but no master objected. The boys welcomed the change of routine when he assured them this was how to build muscles. They all seemed like children to him. None was as old as he had been when he was first admitted, brazenly lying about his age.

Having exhausted his first thirty victims, he began collecting another thirty. He was preempted by Master of Rapiers, Sir Quinn. Quinn often had strange ideas. His current notion was that Badger needed a lesson in Isilondian rapier technique. Badger despised rapiers. He was a saber man, a slasher. He wanted to smite a foe, not poke at him. Nor could he see any reason for learning all the various styles that Ironhall liked to teach when Ironhall's own style was the best. A man who had mastered that could beat any opponent.

Furthermore, he already knew a fair bit about Isilondian-style rapier fencing. To conceal that fact from Quinn he had to play clumsy, which required superhuman reflexes when fencing at that level. By the time the fading light brought the session to an end, he had developed a throbbing headache.

"Excellent, excellent!" Quinn blathered. "We'll make a rapier man out of you yet."

Over Badger's dead body.

Of course his dead body was going to be available quite soon now. . . .

"Prime?" The voice at elbow came from a fuzzy named Audley. His face was wet and he looked worried. "There's something nasty going on in the bath house."

"What sort of nasty?"

"The Brat. It sounds like Servian."

Badger hesitated only a moment. Discipline was Second's responsibility, not his; but Marlon had not reported back yet, and the healing would probably leave him dazed for a while. The Brat was always the newest recruit, who had no name because he had left his old one behind when he was admitted and had not yet chosen another. Hazing the Brat was the juniors' favorite occupation. It was supposed to weed out the weaklings, so the masters usually turned a blind eye; everyone had been the Brat once.

But Audley was a good man, almost ready to hang a sword on and be a senior. If he said "nasty" then it must *be* nasty. Servian had been warned before.

"Thanks." Badger ran.

From the gym to the bath house was no distance, but he was soaked by the time he pounded up the steps. He could hear the kid's screams from there.

It was very nasty, far beyond normal hazing. Servian's meanness was the sort of disease that could infect others and turn them into henchmen. He had three of them with him now. They had the Brat's clothes off; they were holding him down and "cleaning" him with wet sand.

Badger lost his temper.

He waded into all four of them, fists flying. The three disciples were only kids, who could be sent flying with a slap; but Servian himself was a burly, sulky brute, as big as Badger himself. It took a couple of real punches to lay him on the floor, where he belonged.

"Put your clothes on, lad," he told the victim, who was starting to grin through his tears at this rough justice so unexpectedly imposed on his tormentors. Servian tried to rise; Badger pinned one of his hands to the flagstones with a boot, not gently. "You stay there for now. The rest of you, on your feet!" He made a mental note of their names. "Go to your dorms and stay there until I say otherwise. Don't expect to eat tonight.

Do expect more bad things to happen. Run!"

When the weeping accomplices had gone, it was safe to deal with the pervert himself. "Get up! What you should have realized by now, scum, is that the Brat isn't the only one being tested."

Servian scrambled to his feet. For a moment he seemed ready for a second round, but when he saw that his supporters had gone and Badger was willing, he lowered his fists and just scowled.

"What 'ju mean?"

"I mean you're gone, lost, blown. The King has no use for sadists. You can't be trusted with a Blade's skills." It was unfortunate, because horrible Servian had the makings of an excellent swordsman.

Having confirmed that the Brat was more frightened than hurt, Badger sent him off to the infirmary to have his scrapes bandaged, and then marched Servian out to the quad. And over to the stocks. In his four years in Ironhall, he had never seen the stocks used, except sometimes to torment the Brat. He couldn't think of anything else bad enough for Servian at the moment. He rather hoped the thug would resist, but he submitted without a word. Badger locked him in, wrists and neck pinned between the boards, and left him there, standing in the storm. Then he went in search of Grand Master.

Grand Master, it seemed, was looking for Prime.

Badger tried First House, then West House, then back to Main House. They must have missed each other several times, because they were both well soaked when they eventually met. Their encounter took place back in the gym, before an audience of knights who had lingered to chat, plus a few juniors still tidying away equipment. Grand Master was obviously in one of his ogre moods.

Badger was alone, very much alone. Grand Master had a retinue. On one side of him stood Travers and some of his soprano friends; on the other Servian and his three stooges. Servian's face was swelling nicely, but he smirked at Badger as if to remind him of that ancient principle: *The enemy of my enemy is my friend.*

"Prime! You have been using violence on other candidates!"

"I admit I lost my temper, Grand Master. I was rescuing a boy these four were torturing."

"Even if that were true, it would be no excuse."

"There were four of them. Should I have drawn my sword?"

"Insolence! You should have used your authority. You have betrayed the trust placed in you—attacking boys, abusing Candidate Servian by locking him in the stocks." The old man's manner implied that the worst was yet to come. "*And* you deceived Candidate Travers with some nonsensical tale that has started a flood of absurd rumors."

Travers failed to meet Prime's eye. He had not kept the secret.

"I told him the truth." Badger could never understand why the Order had chosen Sir Saxon its Grand Master. He had been a compromise candidate, apparently, but even that did not excuse such a blunder. He always seemed so *small,* although he was quite tall for a Blade. Some days he greeted Badger by name, thumped his shoulder, made jokes, asked his advice. Other days, as now, he spluttered and squeaked like a mad tyrannical bat.

"You did not! You deceived him. You proved unworthy of the honor conferred on you."

Badger cared nothing for the honor of being Prime. He cared nothing for the Order, nor Ironhall and its inhabitants. He never had. "I told him that candidates who elect to leave are picked up by teamsters on the road. I also told him that the Order pays for this mercy, and also finds them work in Prail or Blackwater. Do you deny this?"

The old goat gibbered for a moment. Then, "Who ever told you such nonsense?"

"I have known that for years. I made it my business to find out before I turned up on your doorstep, Grand Master. Even then I knew better than to put myself in a trap that had no way out."

Grand Master grew redder and shriller, while the audience watched in amazement. "This is rubbish! You have betrayed the trust I placed in you when I appointed you Prime."

"You appointed me Prime? By puking Stalwart, you mean?"

"Insolence! Go to your room and stay there until I give you leave!"

Oh, flames! "You are a bucket head," Badger said sadly. "If you must be so petty, why do it in public?" He turned to go.

"And leave your sword!" Grand Master squealed.

Badger went, leaving his sword. He resisted the temptation to leave it in Grand Master. He even resisted the temptation to do to him what he had done to Servian.

Later, sprawled on his cot, he was seriously

tempted to go back down to the hall and correct that mistake. By doing so, he would throw away four years' grinding hard work. He would ruin all his plans. But he would not die after all.

5

Return of the Lost Lamb

"We're almost there!" Wart said cheerfully.

Emerald thought, *And about time!*

Ironhall was a vague something to her left. The rain had almost stopped, but the wind still blew, and the night was far too dark for any sane person to be riding over rocky country like Starkmoor. Of course sanity was an illusive concept when applied to a not-quite-seventeen-year-old-male; and when that man had just become *Sir* Stalwart, member of the White Star, companion in the Loyal and Ancient Order of the King's Blades, official hero, an expert swordsman who had recently won his first mortal duel and been sent on a vital state mission with almost unrestricted authority, sanity was about the last thing to expect. She was cold and battered and one big blister from ankles to hips. But if Master Smarty Warty had thought he could outride her, he now knew better. She had not screamed for mercy once and was not about to start now.

"I smell magic!"

"Right!" he said, sounding either surprised or admiring. "We're passing the Forge."

That was where the boys were bound, she knew, and it spoke to her as the Blades themselves did. No White Sister could ever describe her reaction to a specific sorcery exactly, and *"hot metal"* was as close as she could come to classifying this one. It was something between an odor and a feeling. She could not see the building itself in the darkness, but an octogram that had been in use for several centuries would have a very wide aura.

A few moments later Wart said, "See that light? Grand Master's study. That's where we're going."

Several windows were showing faint glimmers of candlelight, but if he was pointing, she could not see his hand. The packhorse whinnied wearily, smelling stables ahead.

Her life had been *so* peaceful until Sir Snake had interfered in it! Just two weeks ago, she had been a deaconess in the White Sisters' tree city of Oakendown, nearing the end of her training. The nightmare had begun when she was unexpectedly summoned before Mother Superior and sworn in as a full Sister on the spot. Four years' quiet study had been followed by days of mad confusion and mortal peril. She had been rescued in the end by Wart, this peach-faced stripling who had turned out to have so many unexpected skills. She would have been more grateful if he had not helped put her into the danger in the first place.

Yesterday had seemed like the start of a fine new life at court. She had ridden in from Valglorious with Mother Superior in that lady's magnificent coach. Mother Superior had turned out to be a much nicer person than her reputation suggested. She had insisted on going around by Newhurst so that Emerald could visit her mother and break the marvelous news that the family home at Peachyard was to be returned to them. Poverty had turned overnight back to wealth—and that good fortune they owed in large part to Wart.

Was that why she was setting off on another mad adventure with him? She was certainly not doing so just to please the King. In the evening she had supped with the King. Wart had been there, as had Commander Bandit; Mother Superior; Lord Chancellor Roland and his delightful wife, Lady Kate; also the devious Sir Snake. Between the conversation and music, they had planned Wart's mission to investigate the suspected sorcerers' lair in Nythia. Emerald had agreed to accompany him, and she was not certain how that had happened.

Snake—he gave snakes a bad name—had pointed out that Wart would need help from the White Sisters to detect magic. Mother Superior had promised to write to the prioress in Lomouth. She could not send a Sister with him, she had said, because he would be traveling on horseback and almost no White Sister knew how to ride. But the old lady knew very well that Emerald could, because they had discussed such things that morning on the coach ride. And the look she had given Emerald had been a clear invitation to volunteer; whereas that morning she had sounded very much against any more such shenanigans. Wart had said nothing, ignoring Emerald completely, although they had gone riding together at Valglorious. So she had spoken up, admitting that she had grown up with horses at Peachyard. At once the King had asked her to accompany Wart.

And she had agreed. *Not* just because Wart had pulled a face at the idea of having to share his mission with her—she hoped she was not so childish. (Although that might have been a *small* part of it . . .) And *not* just to please the King. She had found Ambrose IV much too big and too loud. He had kept repeating the same joke about Wart and her being the King's Daggers, which everyone had to laugh at. He fancied himself a musician, and the funniest part of the evening had been watching the other guests trying to keep straight faces while he and Wart played duets on their lutes. As a former minstrel, Wart had been tying his fingers in knots in his efforts to follow the King's scrambled keys and timing.

All in all, it had been an exhausting evening. When the party finally broke up, Emerald headed back to the Sisters' quarters with Mother Superior.

"You wanted me to go with Stalwart, my lady," Emerald said. "May I ask why?"

Mother Superior sighed. "Because I am worried about that boy. He did so amazingly well at Quagmarsh! I am afraid it has made him dangerously overconfident. He will get himself killed. He needs someone sensible to look after him." She regarded Emerald with a pair of old but extremely shrewd gray eyes. "And why did you agree to go?"

"For that exact same reason!"

They had both laughed.

After fourteen hours in the saddle, the joke was no longer funny.

Wart dismounted and for once remembered his manners enough to hold Emerald's horse while she did. Faint rays glimmered through a small barred window. Below it was a hitching rail. A latch clattered, hinges creaked, and she followed Wart's silhouette inside.

"This's called the Royal Door," he said. "There's always a light in here. . . ." He took the lantern down off its hook and turned up the wick. The golden glow brightened to reveal a large circular chamber, completely empty except for a narrow stone staircase spiraling up the wall.

"For the King?"

"And other visitors. Ah!" He had found a bell rope. He hauled on it, but the masonry absorbed any sound he may have produced. "Can you come back out and hold the light for me? If he assigns a Blade to someone—an ambassador or a duke, f'r instance—then this is the way they come."

He fussed over the packhorse's load while Emerald held the light for him. She was shivering. Judging by his angry growls, his fingers were too cold to work properly, but eventually he managed to detach one long bundle.

"What about the horses?"

"Small Master will send someone, of course. Come on."

He led the way back inside. Although he must be as tired and sore as she was, he ran up the steps two at a time, eager for the coming interview. She knew he detested Grand Master, who had held despotic authority over him for four years. Was he hoping to get some of his own back? The bell had been heard somewhere, because a door halfway up the stair stood ajar, waiting for them. Pushing it wide, Wart strode forward into the brightness of candles and a crackling fire.

"Stalwart!" Grand Master was not as old as Emerald had expected. His face was bleak and bony, and what flesh there was on it had settled into grooves and lines, but there was no gray in the narrow fringe of beard. He gaped in amazement at his visitor.

"Good chance to you, Grand Master! Glad we didn't drag you out of bed. My companion, Luke of Peachyard. . . ."

Luke? Emerald bristled. Before the Sisterhood renamed her Emerald, she had been Lucy Pillow, but that hated name was supposed to be dead and forgotten. The great Sir Stalwart would scream in fury if she referred to him as Wat Hedgebury! He had not warned her that he expected her to masquerade as a boy. Mother Superior had advised male clothing for comfort on horseback, although she had admitted it would also deflect unwanted questions. Real ladies were expected to travel by coach; other women never had reason to go anywhere. The Sisters had their own priorities.

Grand Master barely spared a glance for "Luke," who must be a child or servant, because he was not wearing a sword. "Good chance to you, Stalwart. This is a pleasant surprise." That was not a lie, just sarcasm. His initial amazement had given way to anger and disapproval. Emerald suspected his face often expressed disapproval; he had that sort of a mouth.

Wart tossed his sodden cloak over a stool. "A surprise to me also. If you would have the horses cared for, please? Do not mention my name."

Grand Master went to the other door and paused with his hand on the latch. "And yourselves? Food? Beds? Are you and the boy staying?"

The *boy* removed her cloak also and headed for the fire to thaw out her hands.

"Can't," Wart said cheerfully. "I must be on my way directly. If you would kindly have replacements saddled up? And one extra mount."

The older man glared at him, but when no explanation followed, he opened the door and stuck his head out to give instructions. Wart joined Emerald at the fire, shivering and rubbing his hands. He did not even look at her, but his eyes were gleaming; he was enjoying himself enormously. She saw him check the hang of his jerkin, making sure the edge concealed the diamond star pinned on his doublet. He went to the table and began untying the long package he had brought.

The room dearly needed a woman's touch. Stone walls and plank floors made it grim; there were cobwebs in the window niches. Its aging furniture was ugly and mismatched, none of it comfortable—a settle by the fireplace, a very ancient leather chair facing it, three stools around a table. Grand Master himself had the same shabby, neglected appearance.

He finished giving orders, closed the door, and went to join Wart at the table. "You bring sad tidings. I should send for Master of Archives."

"No! My presence here tonight must be known only to yourself and one other." The covering of oiled cloth fell open, revealing three swords. Swords coming back to Ironhall meant dead Blades, but Wart now ignored them, donning his most innocent expression, which made him look about twelve and invariably signaled trouble ahead. "To save time, would you be so kind as to summon Candidate Badger?"

Grand Master dropped any pretense of enjoying the evening. "No."

Wart smiled at this show of resistance. "I must insist, Grand Master."

"Not until I know why you want him."

"I need to borrow him for a few days."

"What! Why?"

The smile grew wider. "I am sorry I cannot answer that."

"The charter decrees that all candidates reside within the school until completion of their training."

Confrontation.

Emerald waited to see what Wart would do next. His White Star would probably be enough authority by itself, but she knew that he also carried his commission from the Court of Conjury. That bore the royal seal and identified the bearer as "our trusty and well-beloved Stalwart, companion in our Loyal and Ancient Order of the King's Blades. . . ." It commanded "our servants, officers, vassals, and loyal subjects without exception" to aid him in "all his dread purposes and ventures." With that backing, Wart could practically order Grand Master to jump down a well.

But Grand Master had just noticed the sword dangling at Wart's thigh with its hilt toward him. It bore a cat's-eye stone on the pommel—quite a large one, because it was a rapier, whose point of balance had to be well back toward the user's hand. He had explained all that to Emerald at least twice. He was very proud of his sword, was Wart. He called it *Sleight*.

"Where did you get that?"

Amazingly, Wart's smile could grow even wider, and did. "From Leader." That was the Blades' own name for Commander Bandit. "And he got it from Master Armorer. Didn't they tell you about this, Grand Master?"

The older man's face was red enough to set his beard on fire. He seemed to keep his teeth clenched while he said, "I do not recall your being bound."

"No? Well, that was because Fat Man postponed my binding. Master of Archives has the edict somewhere in the records."

More confrontation.

Obviously Wart was just dying to pull out his commission and smash Grand Master to bits with it. Grand Master, in turn, was wondering how much authority Wart really had. He chose not to take the risk of asking.

"I must know what business you think you have with Prime."

Wart tried to stick out his jaw, but it was not a very convincing jaw yet. "I will explain when he gets here."

Grand Master sighed. "I do not wish to trouble him, you see. Some boys . . . candidates . . . have trouble as they approach their binding. Badger is one of them, I fear, poor lad. He has not been a success as Prime. He has become very jumpy and short-tempered."

"Badger? Never! The man's a rock."

Grand Master shook his head sadly. "You would be quite shocked by the change in him."

Wart said softly, "I will judge him for myself."

Confrontation again. Again it was the older man who yielded.

"I will be present while you speak with him."

Wart shrugged. "I am on the King's business, and I bind you to secrecy by your oath of allegiance."

That was a slight retreat, probably designed to trap the other man into demanding to see his credentials, but Grand Master refused to take the bait.

"And I do not agree that he may accompany you when you leave."

Wart just smiled. Grand Master swung around and went back to the door. Wart closed his eyes for a moment and sighed as if his joy was almost too much to bear. He did not look at Emerald; he might have forgotten she was there.

Having given the orders, Grand Master returned to the table with a thin smile nailed on his face. "Well, well, brother! You must have been having some interesting experiences since you left us so unexpectedly."

If he had been a girl being admitted to Oakendown and in need of a new name, Emerald would have suggested "Minnow"—small, slithery, and skittish. His abrupt reversals told her that he was a water person. Although all the manifest elements—air, fire, earth, and water—were present in everyone, one was always dominant. White Sisters were trained to identify elementals, and only a water person could run through so many moods so quickly. The virtual elements were harder to assess, but she was detecting a strong component of chance, which always seemed to her like a faint rattling of dice being rolled. Water-chance people should never be put in positions of responsibility, but their combination of luck and malleability often won them appointments for which they were totally unsuited.

"Life has been interesting," Wart agreed. "These swords . . . fallen Blades. They all gave their lives for their King." He drew a sword and raised it. "I bring *Woe,*" he proclaimed, "the sword of Sir Beaumont, knight in our Order, who died three days ago at a place called Quagmarsh while serving as a commissioner of His Majesty's Court of Conjury. Cherish this sword in his memory." He sheathed *Woe* and passed it with both hands to Grand Master, who took it the same way.

"It shall hang in its proper place forever."

The confrontation had been set aside for now. These were fellow Blades mourning their brethren.

"You see the hilt is partly melted? He was struck by hellfire." Wart drew another. "I bring *Quester*, the sword of Sir Guy, knight in our Order, who died three days ago at a place called Quagmarsh while serving as a commissioner of His Majesty's Court of Conjury. Cherish this sword in his memory."

Grand Master shuddered and repeated his formula: "It shall hang in its proper place forever. What happened to him?"

"He was trying to save a woman from a chimera."

"Chimera?"

"Magical monster. They vary, depending on the ingredients. They can be quite scary, especially at night; can't they, Luke? This one tore Guy's throat out before Snake got it. By the way . . . news of a brother. Yesterday Snake was promoted from member to officer in the White Star."

"Wonderful!" Grand Master said. "I shall announce that in the hall with great pride."

The falsehood made death elementals flutter on the edge of Emerald's awareness. Inquisitors were not the only ones who could detect lies; most White Sisters could do it too. Grand Master was jealous of Snake's success.

Wart raised the third sword. "I bring *Durance*, the sword of Digby, knight in our Order and First Lord Digby of Chase, Warden of the King's Forests, who died yesterday, struck down by sorcery in the presence of His Majesty."

"What?" Grand Master screeched, ceremony forgotten. "How?"

"That we don't know . . . yet."

"You're serious? Where was the Guard? Who did it?"

"Nobody. I saw it. The whole court saw it. He was stabbed through the heart and there was no one within four paces of him."

Grand Master scowled in disbelief. "That is outrageous!"

"We're working on it."

"This Quagmarsh place—were you there too?"

"Not during the fighting," Wart said with disgust. "Just—"

Knuckles rapped on the door.

6

Pilot on Board

A man stepped in and slammed the door behind him, while fixing a dangerous glower on Grand Master. He was of average height, but heavyset, huskier than any of the Blades Emerald had seen during her brief stay at court. She knew that seniority in Ironhall depended entirely on order of admittance, not on age or ability, and the newcomer sported a murky beard shadow that made him look ten years older than Stalwart. He saw Wart and stiffened. His dark gaze flickered quickly over the cat's-eye sword, the courtly clothes so much more splendid than his own Ironhall rags, the unarmed youth by the fire, the three swords on the table.

"Good chance!" He had a harsh, unmusical voice. "*Sir* Stalwart, I presume?"

Wart made a leg. "The same."

Badger doffed his hat and offered a full court bow. His black and very curly hair was blazoned by a startling white patch right above his forehead. If he had not chosen the name of Badger for himself, the other boys had hung it on him. "Congratulations." He awarded Emerald a second, slower, inspection, then looked back at Wart. "Private?"

"Guard. Until my enlistment becomes official, I am assisting Sir Snake in some confidential matters."

"Indeed!" Badger looked impressed, but Emerald detected a glimmer of something false, a wrongness. "I never believed the lies some dishonest people were spreading around here about you."

"Thank you." Wart was enjoying himself again. "You are not wearing a sword, Prime."

"No, I'm not."

"Grand Master, why is Prime Candidate Badger running around naked?"

The mercurial Grand Master was red with fury again. "A disciplinary matter."

Wart said, *"Tsk!* Then perhaps my timing is appropriate. I came to offer you a break from routine, brother. By the way, over there is my assistant, Luke of Peachyard. Sh—*he* has certain skills that may be useful to me. Candidate Badger, Luke."

Emerald and Badger exchanged nods. This

time his appraisal was even longer, as if something about Luke puzzled him.

Wart and Badger were presently united in baiting Grand Master, but they were very dissimilar people. Either Wart had invented their former friendship, because it suited him to believe in it at the moment, or they were a striking case of opposites attracting. He was an air-time person, which was why he was so incredibly agile with a sword and such a fine musician. Badger was bone and muscle, probably tenacious or at least stubborn, not much humor. . . . Yes, even his name . . . Badger was an earth person, like Emerald herself. And his virtual element? Wart had called him a loner, so not love. Not *chance* by any stretch of the imagination; he was the sort of plodder who calculated every step.

"I'm on my way," Wart said airily, "to investigate a suspected nest of traitor sorcerers, and I know you used to be familiar with the area. There shouldn't be any fighting, just a little snooping and riding around. I'll have you back here in four or five days."

"And did Grand Master say I could go out to play?"

"Grand Master?" Wart asked vaguely. "Oh, yes, Grand Master. Well, I'm sure he will not deny you this opportunity of serving His Maj—Fat Man, I mean. We of the Guard always call him Fat Man. There's nothing Grand Master *can* do about it, really, since the King has forbidden him to expel any more kids without royal permission in writing."

"Indeed?" Badger said thoughtfully. "I don't believe I knew that."

"Leader told me; perhaps I shouldn't have mentioned it. Grand Master, what do you—"

"What is *that*?"

Wart looked down to see where the older man was pointing. "Oh, that!" If he had exposed his star deliberately, it had been very skillfully done and he ruined the effect by blushing. Emerald was certain he had just forgotten to keep it hidden. "A token of His—of Fat Man's appreciation. For services to the Crown."

Badger and Grand Master exchanged looks of amazement.

"Flames and death!" Badger growled. "You must have had a busy couple of weeks, brother Stalwart!"

"It was strenuous at times," Wart said with unusual modesty.

"Well, I am sure Grand Master will not deny you any reasonable request now. He and I could use a break from each other, certainly." Even if

Badger was not much of a humorist, he could help Wart hammer on Grand Master's coffin. "I'll need a sword. I won't come without a sword."

"Of course not. You need a *good* sword. I suppose you still hanker after those wood-chopping sabers? Try this." Wart offered the one he had been holding all this time.

"That sword belongs here!" Grand Master bleated angrily.

Badger hefted it and tried a couple of swings. "A little lighter than I prefer, but very fine!" He peered at the blade. *"Durance?* Whose was she?"

"Digby's."

"Digby? I remember him! Warden of Forests? He gave the Durendal Night speech last year. No, two years ago."

Grand Master tried again. "His sword has been Returned and belongs here!"

"I didn't finish Returning it." Wart gave Badger the scabbard also. "You had not accepted it. Besides, it's Digby's killers we're hunting, so I'm sure he would have been happy to lend us *Durance* for a few days."

"Candidate Badger is not bound!" Grand Master protested. "He is not entitled to wear a cat's-eye sword. Did the King give you permission to hand out cat's-eye swords?"

"Fat Man pretty much gave me a free hand. *Durance* is a good name for a badger's sword."

Badger looped the baldric over his shoulder and adjusted it to fit his thick chest. "I hope I can help her to avenge her master."

There was something about him that set Emerald's teeth on edge. An earth person, certainly. And his dominant virtual? Not love, not chance. And it could not be time, because she was an earth-time person herself, and another would not give her this scratchy, unsettled feeling. That left only death. She had never met any earth-death people; there had been none at Oakendown. They made the finest warriors, of course. Human landslides. Ruthless, probably possessed of unlimited courage. Deadly.

"I'll go and get my cloak and razor," Badger said in his harsh growl. "Meet you downstairs?"

"Be so kind as to send for our horses now," Wart told Grand Master.

The older man seemed to be building up to an apoplectic fit. "By what right do you presume to give me orders?" he roared.

Wart beamed and reached inside his jerkin to produce the scroll with the royal seal. The sight of it was enough. Grand Master muttered an oath. Spinning on his heel, he headed to the door.

Badger smiled for the first time, reflecting Wart's triumphant grin. "What is this place we're going to scout?"

Wart checked to make sure Grand Master was outside. "It's in Nythia. A house called Smealey Hole."

All the color drained out of Badger's face.

7 Nythia

By the time they rode into Prail next morning, Wart was wondering whether Snake's way of traveling was quite as admirable as he had at first believed. Of course Snake would not have lost the trail after leaving Ironhall and thus would not have been forced to wander the moors in a downpour all night. Snake would not have had to put up with Badger's sarcastic comments. Emerald's had been even worse, but by dawn she had stopped speaking to him altogether, which was an improvement. Chilled and exhausted and bad tempered, they came down to the cold gray waters of the Westuary. Not far out from the shore stood a wall of white sea fog, hiding the hills of Nythia beyond.

Possibly some traitorous Nythians still believed that Nythia should be a separate country, but it had been a province of Chivial for centuries, despite many attempted revolutions.

The last uprising, when Stalwart was a child, had been suppressed by King Ambrose in person. He had ridden through the breach at the storming of Kirkwain with his Blades around him, and Ironhall's *Litany of Heroes* included several stirring tales of that campaign.

Nythia was a peninsula. It could be reached by a short ferry trip across the Westuary inlet or by a daylong ride around it. Until very recently any seafarer risked capture and enslavement by Baelish pirates, but now there were strong rumors that a treaty had been negotiated to end the war. The raiding seemed to have stopped, and Digby had reported that ferrymen were willing to risk the crossing again.

The fare had to be bargained over, the baggage loaded, and the horses turned in to a posting house. Badger took care of all that, because he was the least weary of the three of them. He could also look fiercer. Nevertheless, Stalwart was already wishing he had never involved Badger in his mission. He was being much less helpful than expected.

That problem could wait. The boat was small, smelly, and bouncy, but the moment the master and his boy cast off the lines, Stalwart rolled himself up on the deck in his blanket and let the world disappear.

* * *

By afternoon, life had become a little brighter. The sleep on the boat had helped. So had a truly enormous meal at an inn in Buran, where they disembarked. Now the sun was shining and the road was dry, winding through prosperous farmland flanked by rolling green hills speckled with sheep. The horses they had hired were fine beasts and well fitted out. It was time to form a plan of campaign.

Stalwart rode in the middle, keeping the other two apart. When they had been properly introduced, Badger had remarked that honorable warriors did not take women along on dangerous missions and ladies did not dress like that. Emerald had been snarling and snapping at him ever since. He had always been a bit of a churl; becoming Prime seemed to have made him a lot worse, so perhaps there had been something in what Grand Master said.

"Why don't you begin at the beginning again?" he growled. "You weren't making much sense last night."

"I'll use nice short words this time," Stalwart said cheerfully. "The elementaries that sell black magic are mostly located near Grandon or other big cities, because that's where the rich customers are. The sorcerers themselves come from all over. It takes eight of them to chant a spell, and they have to learn their nasty trade somewhere. Snake has discovered that a lot of them were trained by an order that calls itself the Fellowship of Wisdom. It inhabits a house called Smealey Hole."

"On the south edge of Brakwood," Badger agreed, "near Waterby."

"Snake's even found letters hinting that its members organized the Night of Dogs attack. He also suspects that some of the villains who slipped through his nets may have gone back there. The Fellowship is hiding them. So when Lord Digby set off on his tour of the King's western forests, Snake asked him to take a look at Smealey Hole."

Badger snorted disbelievingly. "A peer-over-the-wall look at it or a climb-through-the-pantry-window-at-midnight look at it?"

"Probably a can-you-sell-me-something-to-get-rid-of-my-mother-in-law look at it."

"And that's why he was murdered a week later? Do they kill the minstrel who comes to sing or the tinker who mends pots? Wart, are you quite sure Snake doesn't just want to keep you out of harm's way until you've grown up enough to wear Guard livery without making everyone die laughing?"

"Quite sure. If you don't want to help, go home to Ironhall and wipe the juniors' noses."

"Grand Wizard thinks this new sorcery is a short-range weapon, so all the Old Blades are frantically rounding up suspects around Grandon, but you get blown away to the other side of the kingdom?"

"Grand Wizard is just guessing," Stalwart said with as much confidence as he could summon. "So's Snake, I suppose, but his guesses *work*!"

Badger would not give up. "But you don't know what Digby found at Smealey or if he went there at all."

"We do know he went there. His retinue says so—he had clerks, huntsmen, grooms, and squires with him. But he left them all behind in Waterby and went to Smealey with just one local guide, so we don't know what he saw or who he talked to. He died before he could report to Snake. He didn't mention anything to the King, but he wouldn't, because Fat Man had forbidden him to join the Old Blades."

"Doing-a-favor-for isn't joining."

"Brother, you do *not* argue that sort of point with kings!"

No need to tell Badger that Snake was now in royally hot water. If Digby's death was not explained and avenged very soon, he might find himself in the Bastion, rattling every time he scratched his fleabites.

Badger thought for a while as they cantered along the trail. "If Digby found evidence of treason, why didn't he send a courier to Snake? Why didn't he rush home himself? He can't have found much if he just carried on with his tour, counting antlers hither and yon across Chivial."

"We're puzzled by that. He didn't do either! He went to Smealey on the twelfth. He was expected back in Grandon about the thirtieth, but instead he arrived on the seventeenth. Next day he died. So he did cut his tour short, but not as short as he could have done. Nor did he tell his men why he was in such a hurry to get back."

"If these sorcerers were so frightened that Digby was going to tattle bad stories about them, why would they not just have someone put an arrow through him in the forest? Why do anything as risky as putting a curse on him?"

"He was not cursed!" Emerald shouted. "The Sisters would have detected a curse as soon as he entered the palace. This is a new sort of magic."

"And if Wart drops dead when he gets back to Nocare, that will prove it."

Stalwart still held on to his temper. "When

Snake told me about Smealey Hole, I recalled the name. How could I ever forget it? You mentioned it one night when we were juniors. We were discussing secret passages. Orvil told a story about being shown one, then you said that you'd *found* one. You'd been exploring caves, you said, and discovered a man-made tunnel, with steps carved into the rock, and you followed it up to a door. You learned later that this was a smuggler's route, leading into the local lord's house, Smealey Hole."

Badger shrugged. "I don't remember. If I said that, then I was lying. I suppose I thought Orvil was bragging and I could top his story with a better one—we were only kids, remember."

Most of them had been kids, but not him. He'd claimed to be fifteen when he was admitted, but no one had believed him. He'd been shaving, even then.

"You sounded very convincing."

"I'm a good liar. It's quite likely that there is such a passage, so perhaps I'd heard about it and claimed to have seen it. The house is really Smealey *Hall* but it's always known as Smealey Hole, which is the name of the pothole where the Smealey River disappears. There's lots of caves south of Brakwood, and a secret back door is never a bad idea in wild and whiskery country like that. But my home was at Kirkwain, north of the forest. I've never been near Smealey Hole or Waterby. What I do know about the Hole is that there's a curse on it."

"What sort of curse?" Emerald asked, looking skeptical.

"Terrible things happen to people who live there. It's very old, but no family has ever owned it for long. They all die nastily."

"For instance?"

"For instance . . . if you knew the name of Smealey, Wart, you must have recognized Waterby, too. I mean, you'd heard about it before this Digby murder?"

"Just that Durendal was named Baron Roland of Waterby because it was there he saved the King's life."

"You remember what it says in the *Litany*?"

"Of course." Stalwart had heard it read out often enough, like all the other great tales of Blades who had saved their wards' lives or lost their own in trying. Durendal's was special. *"'Number 444: Sir Durendal, who on the sixth day of Sixthmoon, 355, in a meadow outside Waterby single-handedly opposed four swordsmen seeking to kill his ward and slew them all without his ward or himself taking hurt.'* That's the only time a Blade has ever managed four at once," he explained for Emerald's benefit, "and to do it on open ground was just incredible. In a narrow passage—"

"Two of the men he killed," said Badger, "were sons of Baron Smealey of Smealey Hole. Another brother was executed later in Grandon Bastion, but only after he'd murdered his father, the Baron. *That's* the sort of curse I mean."

Stalwart waited for Emerald to comment on the magic of curses, but what she said was, "So it has a long history of treason?"

"Possibly. Look, there's a corner of Brakwood now!" Badger pointed at hills ahead.

Although Brakwood was a royal forest, it was not an unbroken expanse of trees from Waterby to Kirkwain. It was rough country, partly wooded, partly open; most of it hilly, none of it cultivated. It included lakes and rivers. It all belonged to the King, who would come and hunt there every three or four years. He allowed no one else to do so, or even to cut wood without his permission. Enforcing the unpopular forest laws was the responsibility—and principal headache—of Lord Florian, the Sheriff of Waterby, and it was to him that Stalwart must look for assistance in his mission.

Snake's instructions had been simple enough.

"You proved your courage at Quagmarsh. I do *not* want heroics this time, understand? *Don't* go blundering into Smealey Hole yourself, or we'll have two deaths to investigate. Just track down that local guide who escorted Digby there. Find out from him whom Digby saw and what was said. Then talk around. Find out all you can about the Fellowship. If you can lay your hands on evidence of black magic—at least two independent witnesses—send a courier posthaste back here, and I'll bring the Old Blades at a gallop. At *that* point you can start to scout out the country, so you can help us plan our attack."

Then Snake had skewered Stalwart with a glittery stare. "Can I trust you to take your commission along? Theoretically, that gives you almost unlimited power, you know. It would let you put the Sheriff and all his men under your command and go in with swords flashing. Try anything like that, my lad, for any reason short of absolute proof of treason and an imminent attack upon His Majesty, and I'll feed you alive to the palace rats!"

Snake had described Waterby as a pleasant little town on the Brakwater. It had long since recovered from the siege of 355, he said, but its walls had never been rebuilt; instead the stones had been put to use in a considerable enlargement of the castle. As the Stalwart expedition rode along the river meadow—probably passing the very spot where Durendal had worked his miracle thirteen years ago—that grim edifice seemed to grow ever more menacing, looming higher over the houses clustered below its towers.

"Master Luke," Stalwart said, "the castellan may board us with the men-at-arms. You'd better dress up as a girl pretty soon."

"The sooner the better. How can you wear these awful clothes all the time?"

"I'd be a wondrous weird swordsman in yours. You, brother, ought to be *Sir* Badger with that sword."

Badger thought for a moment. "'Suppose. Can't see how not."

"Isn't it illegal," Emerald asked, "for any man except a Blade to wear a cat's-eye sword?"

"Very," Stalwart admitted. "No one except snarly old Grand Master will object to Digby's sword helping avenge his murder, but a candidate should not be passing himself off as a companion." Giving Badger the sword might have been a mistake, although a reasonable one, because all other swords in Ironhall were kept blunter than shovels. By wearing it he was committing a major imposture, a crime that could in theory bring the death penalty. The entire Order would scream like rabid dragons. Wart's own status as the first unbound Blade in history was scandalous enough, although it was backed by royal edict and Leader's approval.

"Then introduce him just as plain Badger of Kirkwain, and let everyone jump to the wrong conclusion. And exchange swords."

"Huh?"

She sighed as if he were being unspeakably stupid. "Surely there would be very little objection if *you* carried Lord Digby's sword?"

"Just about none."

"And surely you can lend yours to Badger?"

The men exchanged thoughtful glances. Badger pulled one of his sour smiles. "How can you stand it, brother?"

"Nice bit of hairsplitting," Stalwart agreed, grinning at Emerald to show he was actually grateful. "Let's try that."

Durance and *Sleight* were drawn, exchanged, hefted, swung.

Frowns were frowned, pouts pouted.

"All right if you want to chop meat," Stalwart said. He detested sabers. He was built for speed, not strength.

"Useful if you need to darn socks," Badger countered.

Sleight went back to her owner and *Durance* to the imposter.

"Nice idea," Stalwart told Emerald, "but really good swordsmen like me are all rapier men; Badger's just a blacksmith—beef and no brain. You're right about names, though. Brother, you'll be Master Badger of Kirkwain. If anyone gives you titles, pretend not to notice. Keep the hilt under your cloak whenever possible. And let me do the talking."

"I shall be silent and invisible, Great Leader." Badger pulled his hat down over his eyes.

They rode through the town to the castle. The road ended abruptly at a very smelly moat, a canal from the river. It was spanned by a drawbridge guarded by men-at-arms bearing pikes, but they made no move to challenge the strangers riding through. Hooves drummed on the planks of the bridge, then echoed in the low tunnel through the barbican. Passing under the grisly portcullis and through a final massive door, the visitors emerged into the sunlit bailey. This was a busy little town square in its own right, with washing being dried, horses groomed, men-at-arms drilled, and various wares sold from stalls. Amid all that, women gossiped, men argued, children screamed, dogs barked, and pigeons cooed.

The newcomers barely had time to dismount in front of the door of the keep before a crowd congealed around them to gape. Boys came running to take the horses. A chubby man in servants' garb hurried out, wiping his hands on his apron. He bowed—to Badger, naturally. He probably thought Stalwart was his squire.

"My lords . . . Cuthbert the steward is not available. I am the bottler, Caplin. May I be of assistance?"

Stalwart said, "Pray inform the Sheriff that Sir Stalwart is here and would hold converse with him."

The bottler bowed again, but to the space between the two, as if uncertain which was which. "I will see if his lordship is available, Sir Stalwart."

Badger roared. *"He had better be!* We come on urgent business for His Majesty."

Flustered, Caplin backed away a few steps, then turned and scurried indoors.

"I told you to keep your mouth shut!" Stalwart said bleakly, being careful not to shout. Wrong, wrong, all wrong! Badger's blustering was how a royal official would normally behave, but Snake had sent Stalwart on this mission because he knew how to be inconspicuous. Badger's bellow had been overheard by so many onlookers that the news that the King's men had arrived would be all over the town in an hour. The Fellowship would be sure to have spies near the Sheriff.

8 The Sheriff of Waterby

As a page led the visitors across a gloomy dining hall filled with plank tables and benches, Emerald found her chance to poke Wart in the ribs. He nodded without speaking. The boy disappeared up a very narrow spiral staircase built into the wall of the keep. Wart gestured Badger to go first, then for her to follow. She held back until Badger had disappeared.

"He's betraying you!" she whispered. "When he shouted at the bottler, that was deliberate mischief. Not quite a lie, but I'm sure he's playing you false."

Wart, surprisingly, did not look surprised. He pushed her forward and came up the steps after her, as close as it was possible for two people to go together in that cramped space. "What has he said that's not true?" he asked her shoulder.

"I can't be certain," she told his hat. Badger's dominant element confused her ability to detect falsehood. He had confessed to being a good liar; he might have been joking, but any death person must be a good liar. "But I don't think he's from Kirkwain. Why is he doing this?" She passed a loophole that let in a little light; she wondered if anyone had ever shot arrows out of it, and marveled at the thickness of the wall.

"He's always been sort of surly," Wart said sadly. "He may be jealous of my success. It can't have anything to do with Digby, Sister. It just can't! Any crimes Badger committed before he came to Ironhall are forgotten and will be automatically pardoned when he's bound. For four years, he's had no contact with the world, and why would he spend all that time there if he did not want to be a Blade?"

"Digby went there two years ago."

"Just to give the Durendal Night speech. As I recall, his was even duller than most. Badger and I were only beansprouts then. They keep the riffraff away from important visitors."

The logic seemed inescapable: Whatever was troubling Badger could have nothing to do with Wart's mission. The sound of boots up ahead suddenly stopped. She hurried.

"There you are!" Badger said as she reached him. Did he suspect that she suspected him? The White Sisters did not advertise their ability to detect falsehood, but it must be known in Ironhall.

"The stair's making me giddy."

He turned to continue and she followed. It wasn't the stair making her head spin, she realized—it was magic, growing stronger with every step she climbed. She opened her mouth to shout a warning. But then there was light, and an open door, with the page holding it for her.

Emerald followed Badger in and Wart came at her heels. The boy departed, closing the door. The solar was located high in the keep, with large windows facing safely inward, overlooking the bailey. Sunshine alone would have warmed it comfortably by that time in the afternoon, for it was a small chamber, but the huge fire blazing on the hearth had heated it almost beyond endurance. Incredibly, the sole inhabitant was hunched in a chair directly in front of this inferno. It seemed a wonder that he did not burst into flames himself. He was swaddled in thick robes, wrapped in blankets. His sparse hair was white; his face was hollowed by a loss of teeth, and wrinkled like cedar bark. Obviously Lord Florian was a very sick man; he was also the source of the magic.

Emerald detected healing spells as a sickly-sweet odor. They were all much the same—air and water, a little fire, and much love to nullify the opposing death element—but this mixture represented a very unbalanced octogram, and she always found it unsettling.

Wart was bowing and introducing himself. He did not name his companions.

The Sheriff turned his face from the fire to peer at him with dull, rheumy eyes. "So the King sends children now?" He spoke in a hoarse, painful whisper, barely audible over the logs' crackling.

Wart, who was already turning pink from the heat, turned even pinker. "I repeat: I am a Blade in the Royal Guard, and on His Majesty's business as a commissioner of the Court of Conjury. Here is my warrant."

Florian waved the scroll away with a frail, age-spotted hand. Once he must have been a towering and imposing man, probably a very handsome one, for the bones of his face were craggy. Now he was a ruin, a heap in a chair.

"I care not for your fancy seals and parchment," he whispered. "What does the King want of me now? I have kept his peace here these thirteen years, gathered his taxes, hanged men who took his deer. Must he harass me now, in my last days?"

Badger and Emerald had gone to stand beside the windows, but even there the heat was stifling. To see the Sheriff's face, poor Wart must stay close. He shifted uneasily from foot to foot.

"My lord, the Warden of the King's Forests visited here nine or ten days ago."

"Digby. Known him for years. Comes around every year or two and makes a thorough nuisance of himself. He was underfoot during the rebellion, too. Don't recall he ever did any good then either. He stayed two days and left by the Buran road. Get to the point." Florian's memory was in better shape than the rest of him.

"Day before yesterday he was murdered."

Pause. The old man stared hard at Wart. "So?" he croaked.

"We have reason to believe that his death was connected with his visit here, specifically with the so-called Fellowship of Wisdom." Wart's face was streaming sweat.

"Why? Why do you think that, boy, eh?"

"I am not at liberty to reveal that information, my lord. Lord Digby visited Smealey Hole, or Hall, while he was here?"

"Yes."

"And who went with him?"

"Rhys, one of my foresters. Sent him to make sure Digby didn't get lost or cause trouble." His voice sounded as if it were bubbling through gruel. Why didn't he cough and clear it?

Emerald wished she could warn Wart about

the healing magic. If it came from the sorcerers of Smealey Hole, then Lord Florian was probably in their power, just as her father had been bespelled in his final illness by the enchanters of Gentleholme.

"And what happened?" Wart persisted.

"He talked with the Prior and came back here." *Bubble.*

"That's all? Do you know what they discussed?"

"No. And I don't care."

"I want to speak with this Rhys Forester."

"Well you can't." *Bubble.* "He went off somewhere—" *gurgle* "—couple' a' days ago. Want him myself. Can't find him. Run off after some—" *glug, glug* "—girl, most like. Have him whipped when he shows up." *Gurgle.*

Emerald watched Wart's eyes light up.

"So two men went to the Hole. One has been murdered and the other has disappeared. Is Rhys in the habit of disappearing for days at a time?"

For a long moment the dying Sheriff just sat and made his horrible bubbling noises. Finally he said, "No."

"Has he parents or friends who might know—"

"Pestilence, boy, you're talking rubbish! Young mud-head! Just like Digby. He came back here frothing about raiding the Hole and arresting the brethren, lock, stock, and barrel!" Anger seemed to give Florian strength to ignore his drowning lungs. "Wanted me to call up my Yeomanry and send them in! Had to tell him that Smealey Hole wasn't in the forest, so he'd no authority over it. No one's lodged any complaints of black magic, so can't invoke the Suppression of Magic Act either. There's laws in Chivial, I tell you! And they don't allow arbitrary house . . . searches—" He crumpled into a long paroxysm of painful coughing and spitting. Eventually he gasped, "Stupid idiot!"

Emerald stole a look at Badger, beside her, but Badger was an earth person. "Inscrutable" didn't begin to describe Badger. Wart was beaming, because Snake's guess had been proved right. Digby *had* discovered something suspicious at the Hole. Perhaps he had just asked to buy black magic and the sorcerers had sold him something. Whether that something worked or not would not matter; purveying anything purported to be black magic was a crime. Emerald kept frowning warnings, still wanting to tell him about the healing spell on the Sheriff.

Then Wart showed that he had thought of it for himself. "Tell me about this Fellowship, my lord. You say it isn't known for black magic

Does it do good works, then, like healing?"

"No," Florian mumbled. "Mind their own business, don't poach the King's beasts, pay their taxes and their bills. I got no cause to bother them." He still might have cause to protect them.

"I thank you for your time, my lord," Wart said with a bow. "If I wish to go and speak with the Prior, who will provide me with a horse and a guide?"

Florian stared at the fire for a while as if he had not heard, but at last he whispered. "See Mervyn."

The visitors left him as they had found him, huddled in his chair, slowly dying in front of the fire.

9 Stalwart Sends a Message

Wart halted at the bottom of the stairs, and for a moment just stood there, staring across the dining hall as if wondering where the stench of boiled cabbage came from. Maids were laying out wooden platters and mugs, but no one paid heed to the strangers. Emerald could tell he was excited; he was taut as a lute string.

"I have everything Snake needs for a raid on the Hole," he said. "Digby wanted to do it, so he must have found something seriously wrong. The forester witness has disappeared. Lord Florian is incompetent and perhaps in the traitors' power. That's enough evidence."

Badger groaned. "You only have Florian's word for it that Digby wanted to stage a raid, and you admit that he's too sick to be trusted. He may be hallucinating. Anyway, Digby had the brains of a pony; he probably wanted to play Old Blade all by himself. You have absolutely no reason to believe that Forester Rhys has been murdered."

Wart pouted. Emerald tried not to grin. This was a classic case of an air person wanting to fly and an earth person holding him down. Yet Badger's death dominant still troubled her. Death people were dangerous to both others and themselves. She could imagine him as a great rock that might stand a whole lifetime, poised but unmoving, or might come crashing down at any minute to destroy everything it encountered.

He was certainly persistent. "If Digby really did find evidence of treason or black magic at the Hole and the Sheriff blocked him, then why didn't he rush home posthaste? Or write to Snake?"

"Maybe he did," Emerald said. "Write to Snake, I mean. If you wanted to do that now, Wart, how would you send the letter?"

Wart's scowl turned to a wicked leer of triumph. "I'd give it to someone here in the castle—the castellan or that bottler man or the steward. And he'd probably hand it to the marshal, who'd pass it on to the sergeant-at-arms or the stable manager . . . and eventually a boy on a horse would carry it down to the ferry at Buran. There he'd give it to the boatman, or perhaps take it across to Prail. It would go to the Royal Mail office in Lomouth, so it could travel on the mail coach or by special courier. . . . That's if it ever left Waterby Castle! Or the courier died on the road, maybe. *Digby's letter never arrived!"*

"And Digby?" she asked. "He wouldn't think of that, but he would want to hurry home and deliver a report in person as well. But he daren't neglect his duties, in case the King took offense at his meddling. On the other hand, he wouldn't dally to socialize. So he'd make a very quick trip, but not posthaste. And that's exactly what he did."

Now it was Badger who was frowning, but he did not dispute her logic. "So what do you do now, *Leader*? Write to Snake?"

"That doesn't work!" Wart said, grinning dangerously. "There are traitors right here in Waterby Castle. I send you, Brother Badger."

Even an earth person could show astonishment sometimes. "Me? Grand Master will lay duck eggs!"

"Leave Grand Master to me. Go to Grandon, Candidate Badger, and find Snake, wherever he is. Failing him, report to Durendal—if a sheriff's incompetent, that's the Lord Chancellor's business, isn't it? And take care! You may need your

Ironhall skills on the road. That sword will get you the best mounts in the—"

Badger's always squarish face seemed to develop more stubborn planes and angles. "No. It won't work, Sir Wart. I'll never make it. The law says any man wearing a cat's-eye sword must be able to show a scar over his heart. You've got that fancy commission with the King's seal, but I don't. I'm not wearing Guard livery. I'm not attending a ward. Why not go yourself?"

Emerald knew that that would never do. Wart wanted to snoop around Smealey Hole and get into trouble: fight monsters, kill traitors, be a hero again. He reached in his jerkin and brought out his precious star. "Then take this. That's enough authority to get you into the King's bedroom if you want."

Badger stared at the glittering bauble with wide eyes. He took it as if it were a dangerous scorpion. "These jewels are worth a fortune, Wart! How do you know I won't just steal it?"

"Don't be ridiculous." Wart strode off across the hall with fast strides, making the others run to catch him. "Let's go find this Mervyn the Sheriff mentioned. Hope you don't mind a few more days in those same clothes, because I'm going to sneak you out of here. We'll say we're all heading over to the Hole; when I give you the signal, you turn around and tear down the Buran road before anyone can move to stop you!"

Badger caught Emerald's eye and now the two earth people were in complete agreement: Wart was flying.

10 Mervyn

Emerald knew that Wart could be almost as devious as his hero, Snake. It was no coincidence that the name he had given his sword, *Sleight*, was similar to Snake's *Stealth*. She just hoped that he had some hidden purpose in giving Badger the star, because the more she saw of the man the less she was inclined to trust him.

After several inquiries, Wart was directed to an obscure corner of the bailey, to a tiny shed sporting a dozen or more sets of weathered antlers. Emerald and Badger peeked over his shoulders as he peered in the doorway. The gloomy inside was packed to the ceiling with bows, rods, spears, arrows, nets, mounted heads, horse tack, horns, stuffed birds, sample branches of a dozen different trees, a boar's skull with tusks attached, stuffed birds, and mysterious sacks. Three white-muzzled dogs sprawled asleep underfoot, and the cubicle reeked of animal. In the center of this midden stood a small, bent, white-haired man wearing the green garments of a forester. He had the customary horn hung on his belt, too. What he could actually be doing in there was a mystery, because there was barely room for him to stand, let alone move anything.

"I was told to speak with someone called Mervyn."

The ancient blinked at him. "Eh?"

Wart raised his voice. "The sheriff told me to see someone called Mervyn."

"Ah, he ain't the man he was 'fore his wife died." The forester shook his head sadly.

"Who isn't?"

"Ah, who is?"

"Are you he?"

"Who? What? Speak up, boy, you sound like a wood dove."

The back of Wart's neck was turning pink as he decided that the Sheriff had palmed him off on a doddering antique. He shouted, "Where can I get horses to go to Smealey Hall?"

"Horses live in stables, boy."

"And who'll give them to me?"

"No one. You buy your own horses."

"Do you know a forester named Rhys?"

"That's a cheeky question, boy. Very cheeky.

You think I'm so old you can come 'round here making fun of an old man who's been at his trade these three score years and more, almost four score?"

Emerald was having trouble suppressing a snigger.

"I'm not making fun of you!" Wart howled. "Do you know where Rhys is?"

"Didn't sell it! He was proud of it, you hear?"

"Proud of what?"

"Speak up, boy. Stop mumbling."

"Tell him," Emerald whispered in Wart's ear, "that you think Rhys was murdered."

"Eh?" said the old man sharply. "What's that about murder?"

Deafness could only be carried so far, evidently.

"Rhys guided Lord Digby to Smealey Hall," Wart said in quieter tones, "and Lord Digby has been murdered. The King sent me to find out why, and I want to speak with Rhys."

"He's disappeared," the forester said sulkily. "But he's a good boy and it ain't right what Sheriff says about him selling the horn and going off drinking or chasing women. Wouldn't do that, Rhys wouldn't. He's a fine lad and I says so even if he is my grandson."

"I'm afraid he may have been murdered, too."

Mervyn nodded sadly. "So'm I." Suddenly he advanced on his visitors so that they backed away, into the light. He stood in the doorway and looked them over. "You're the King's men. They said the baby one was in charge. Name of Stalwart. A Blade."

Wart showed his sword. "This is Badger—this is Luke. The King sent us, Forester. If your grandson's been hurt, we'll see that the criminals hang. What were you saying about a horn?"

"He guided earl there. Lordship gave him a horn. It's seemly for lords to reward good service, isn't it? Fine bull horn with gold 'round the top, tooled leather strap. Blows a lovely call, it do. Rhys got lungs! Could hear the boy all the way to Kirkwain on that horn. He wouldn't sell it for all the gold in Chivial."

Wart glanced up at the sun, which was dipping behind the castle wall. "I'm sure he wouldn't. How far is it to Smealey Hole?"

"'Bout a league."

"North?"

"An' a bit west."

"You know if there's more than one way in?"

"And why wouldn't I know?" the old man said indignantly, drawing himself up as straight as he could. "Me being bred and buttered in Brakwood, lived here more'n four score years?

You want to go and root out those sorcerers, boy?"

"I'd like to go and take a look at the place."

"Why didn't you say so sooner?" From somewhere the old man produced a green cap with a pheasant feather in it. He stuck this on his head and set off across the bailey, head down, at a lightning-fast shuffle. The dogs snored on unheeding.

After a day and a half in the saddle, the last thing Emerald wanted to see again was the backs of a horse's ears. The second last thing was Wart blundering into trouble because she wasn't there to warn him. If she complained, he would just leave her behind, so horse's ears it would have to be. She was going to remain Master Luke for a while yet.

At the stables old Mervyn shot off orders like an archer firing arrows. "Patches for him, Snowbird for Sir Stalwart. You've not been skimping on his oats, have you? And Daydream for this one. Fine gentle ride she has. I'll try Daisy, see what you've done to her." The hands jumped to obey.

In the confusion of choosing saddles and watching the fresh horses being readied, Emerald managed to sidle close to Wart at a moment when Badger was out of earshot. "You are a flaming air-head! Why did you give him that star? If he's a traitor, you'll never see it again. It's worth a fortune!"

"It's not worth as much as my life," he said glumly. "Or the King's. Do you think I'd ever let Badger have it if I didn't trust him?"

"You mean you *do* trust him?"

"Y . . . es," Wart said warily. "I think Grand Master's gotten to him. He wouldn't be the first Prime who got driven up a tree by that nump. But I've known Badger for years, Em. If he says he'll do something, he'll do it. He's solid as a rock."

"Perceptive of you to see that. Your brooch is worth a fortune. He'll be set for life."

"He'll be hanged for larceny, you mean." Wart was watching the horses, avoiding her eye. "I'm giving him a chance to show his stuff. If he staggers into the palace, dead on his feet and shouting treason and foul play, he's going to come to Snake's attention, and Leader's. Durendal's, perhaps. Even the King's. It's a *big* chance for him!"

"Do you trust him or don't you?"

Wart shrugged. "Well, yes! Of course. Sort of. Here comes your horse, Luke."

11 The House of Smealey

Old Mervyn set a cracking pace; the horses thundered through the barbican, over the drawbridge, and up into the town. Dogs, pigs, and chickens fled in noisy alarm; pedestrians leaped to safety. In moments the riders had left the houses and were out in open country, lit by a low sun ahead. Wart gave Badger a sign; Badger nodded without a smile, and turned his mount away to head back to Buran and the ferry. The old man did not seem to notice that one of his charges had departed; he rode as he walked, with his head well down. It was almost in the horse's mane.

Although the plain was wide and fertile, the river forced the trail steadily northward, toward wooded bluffs on their right. The old man cut the pace before he winded the horses, and then Wart was able to pull Snowbird alongside and shout a conversation.

"Tell me about this Fellowship of Wisdom, grandfather."

"Don't know nothing 'bout them, lad. Standoffish lot. Teachers, so they say."

"Do they sell conjurations—good-luck charms, healing?"

"Not so's I've heard."

Was he telling the truth or defending a bespelled Sheriff?

"You don't go there much?"

"Nobody does, lad. Haven't been there in ten years. Foresters don't go, even. It's near the forest, not in it." After a brief pause, Mervyn added, "Saw lot of swordsmen around, Rhys said. Sheriff keeps the King's peace! Why'd a gabble of enchanters need swordsmen around?"

As if he timed the interruption for maximum annoyance, he then turned Daisy off the main trail onto a rough path that disappeared into the steep bluffs on the right. Daisy was a very fat mare, almost as old as he was from the look of her, and she made little speed on the slope. Only when the track emerged in open parkland up on the bench, could Stalwart urge Snowbird alongside again.

"How many swordsmen?"

"A score or more, he said."

Bad odds. "What else did Rhys tell you? This was when he went there with Lord Digby?"

"Aye. Nothing much, lad. He was left outside while his haughtiness went in to talk with them. Boy said the swordsmen stood guard on him as if they didn't want him snooping. Not that he would have, of course. Honest lad—"

"Did Digby say anything when he came out? Did he seem angry, or frightened . . . ?"

"Boy said he was white, like he'd had a real shock. He wasn't talking, though. Didn't say hardly a word all the way back to Waterby; lad couldn't tell if he was mad or scared, his wife says."

"Rhys is married?" Stalwart had thought they were discussing someone of his own age.

"Got three sprats," the forester said proudly. "Eight great-grandchildren I got now. His three, and—"

"But as far as you know, the brothers are good and loyal subjects of the King?"

Mervyn rode in silence until Stalwart repeated the question. His deafness seemed to come and go according to his mood. He shot Stalwart a scornful look.

"How can they be, living in that house?"

The house was more important than its inhabitants now. Stalwart must become familiar with the surroundings so he could lead the Old Blades in.

"Tell me about the house."

"Ah!" the old man said, launching his tale with every sign of intending to enjoy the telling of it. "There's a curse on it, there is! Bad place. Been lots of families own it, but never for long. Baron Modred, now . . . well he got it from his father, Gwyn. Gwyn came from out west aways, somewhere around Ghyll. Rough type—said to have been a highwayman or worse. There's tales 'bout him. . . ." He told some. Obviously Gwyn of Ghyll had been born with poison fangs and gone to the bad thereafter. "There was a real Earl of Smealey back then. I wooed one of his serving maids for a while. Married a soldier, she did, and much good—"

"The Earl of Smealey?" Stalwart prompted when he could get a word in.

"No saying what happened to him, exactly. River runs right under the windows, see? Smealey River. It runs down the Hole and never comes up. Water probably joins the Brakwater underground—least, that's what Sheriff thinks—but *things* don't even come back up. Like bodies. No saying how many bodies gone down there in the last few hun'red year."

"The Earl's was one of them?"

"Who can say, see? Gwyn claimed he won the house at dice. Leastways he moved in and nobody felt like moving him out. Started callin' himself the earl. Nobody else did, 'cept to his face. Then came the uprising of 308. First time I handled a sword, that was." Mervyn sighed nostalgically, without saying which side he had fought for. "Gwyn pretended to join and then sold it out. Or else he saw which way the tide ran. An'ways, he betrayed the leaders. The old king created him Baron Smealey for that."

"He sounds utterly charming," Emerald remarked on his other side.

"Aye, that he was, lass," Mervyn agreed, and carried on without showing any awareness that he had supposedly been addressing a boy named Luke. "He had two sons and a bushel of daughters. Eldest was another Gwyn. He and his father died in . . . around 320, must of been. In same night, so they say."

"Did they also die of too much proximity to the river?" Stalwart asked.

"Who knows, when there were no bodies to examine? The second son was Modred, who became the second baron. Had several wives."

"One at a time?"

"Mostly. River's good for divorce, too. Bred

seven sons. Ceri was eldest."

Stalwart knew he ought to recognize that name, but he was distracted by the landscape, realizing that it was a very good site for an ambush. The valley had become a canyon—enclosed by rocky walls and shadowed now, as the sun set. The floor was tufted with scattered trees and enough scrub to hide several dozen swordsmen. Was the old man leading him into a trap? He considered the timing, and decided it would have been impossible for Lord Florian to order any such betrayal at such short notice. If there was going to be treachery, it would happen when he went back to Waterby. He would have to sleep with his eyes open. He hoped Badger had made a safe getaway.

"Is this the main road into Smealey Hole?"

Mervyn pouted at having his reminiscences interrupted. "No. This is back door I'm showing you. Not many know of it. Main road comes in from the east, fords the Smealey. Mustn't do that too near the Hole, see?"

"Of course not. Tell me about Ceri."

"Was ringleader in uprising of 354. Folks hereabout figured they worked it out between them—the boy would raise rebellion while his father crawled around King Ambrose, kissing his horseshoes. That way, whichever way things went, one of them would come out on top and rescue the other."

This tied in with Badger's story. "Then it was Ceri and one of his brothers that Durendal slaughtered when they tried to kill Ambrose outside Waterby?"

"Naw, that was Kendrick and Lloyd, other brothers. Another of the seven, Edryd, died in the siege of Kirkwain."

"Then what did happen to Ceri?"

"Well, after the rebels lost, he was an outlaw for a while, roaming the hills. Till he made the mistake of dropping home for a bite of food and a chat, that is."

"He went down the Hole, too?"

"He'd have been better off," Mervyn said sourly. "His father sold him to King Ambrose. They say the price he got was his own head left on his shoulders. That an' his lands."

"So Ceri was executed?"

"Beheaded in the Bastion, side by side with Aneirin."

"Another brother?" Badger had mentioned only one brother dying in the Bastion.

Mervyn nodded with the satisfaction of a storyteller whose tale has reached a fitting conclusion. "Aneirin was second son. He murdered Modred for betraying Ceri, you see. Strangled his own father with his bare hands! That pretty much finished the line of Gwyn."

Stalwart counted on his fingers. "Two Gwyns, one Modred, then Ceri, Aneirin, Edryd, Kendrick, and Lloyd." That put the score at: Curse eight, Smealeys two. "You left two unaccounted for."

The old man shrugged. "There were a couple'a kids left over. Don't know what happened to them. The Crown seized the lands. They say King thought of using the house as a hunting lodge, decided was too risky—the curse'd get him. Eventually he put it up for sale and yon bunch of sorcerers bought it."

It was as gruesome a tale as Stalwart had ever heard. "How well do you know the grounds right close to the house?"

The old man nailed him with his usual shrewd stare. "Told you I hadn' been here for ten years or more. As a kid I hung around some, courting that girl I told you about." He shrugged.

Wart laughed. "And a bit of poaching."

"Maybe."

"I won't tell the Sheriff. How much do you know about the secret passage?"

"What secret passage?"

"I was told that it was common knowledge

that a secret passage—" That did not make much sense. "There's a back door from Smealey Hole into a cave."

"First I heard of it. Doesn't mean there isn't one, though. Whoa, boy! Here's the Hole."

12 The Hole

Stalwart realized that he had been shouting louder than ever, because a dull roaring had added itself to the problem of Mervyn's deafness. Mist laid a chill dampness on his face. The sides of the valley had been rising steadily, and now the ground fell away precipitously right in front of him. The deeper canyon continued on, curving so that its extent could not be seen; it was no wider but it held a river. Coming into sight around the bend, the stream was darkly smooth; soon it frothed over white rapids, vanished in a clear fall into the great pit almost directly under his toes. No wonder nothing ever reappeared! Anything that went down there would be smashed to fragments in the cavern below.

"Not far to the house," Mervyn bellowed. "You can take a look without being seen. Come on, I'll show you."

Without waiting for an answer, he urged old Daisy down the slope and disappeared. Stalwart's mount declined to commit suicide, balking, tossing its head, backing away. To his intense fury, Emerald easily persuaded her horse to follow the old forester, so she disappeared also.

"You," Stalwart said through clenched teeth, "are going to go down there if I have to carry you! In pieces!" He drew *Sleight*. A rapier made a very good riding crop, because it was flexible and had no cutting edge. In this case he did not even need to use it; he demonstrated the swishing noise it could make, and Snowbird whinnied surrender and agreed to proceed.

There was a path of sorts, but slippery with moss and tangled with ferns. It angled northward at first, down the steep slope to the canyon wall, and then became even steeper, a ledge with a sheer face above and the ghastly maw of the Hole below. The worst part came after that, when it reached water level and the rapids. Cold spray blew in his eyes and the horse's, while a terrible roar echoed back and forth until he thought the noise would burst his skull. At that point there was little pretense of a road, just rocks scoured clean and smooth by the river, part of its bed when it was in spate.

The passage was obstructed by tangles of driftwood. On his left rose a carved and polished wall of stone, sculpted into fantastic niches and pillars; on the other side white water fell away into nothing.

Why had he ever gone to Ironhall? Why hadn't he stayed a minstrel?

Worse, Emerald had stopped, blocking the way. Old Mervyn was past the horrors and waiting for them up ahead, perceptibly higher than they were. From him the river fell, swirling and leaping, raising white cockscombs against the rocks, spinning in dark whirlpools. Just behind Stalwart, it disappeared altogether. . . . His horse was trembling even harder than he was.

It was not a good place for a chat.

Emerald looked around, her eyes wide. She shouted something. He saw her mouth move, but could hear nothing. He yelled back to demonstrate. She understood, and pulled her right foot out of her stirrup as if she was going to dismount.

"Don't!" Stalwart screamed. "You're crazy!"

There was no room for such nonsense. The horses were growing more terrified by the second. If one hoof slipped on the slick-wet rocks, the Hole was going to have two more victims, or even four. Fortunately Emerald worked that out and let her horse proceed up the slope, out of that madness.

The path continued upriver, still too narrow for two horses abreast, while the noise gradually dwindled behind them. The trail rose higher above the water as it rounded the bend of the canyon and entered a wide valley, bereft of real trees but shaggy with brush and saplings. Mervyn reined in and pointed a bony hand at a knoll some distance ahead. Its river side was a cliff, but the rest of its slopes seemed gentle enough. It bore buildings on its crest.

"Smealey Hole," he explained needlessly, then scowled at Emerald. "What was wrong with you, lass, back there? All that tomfoolery?"

"There's something down there," she said, speaking to Stalwart. "I can't see what it is, but I know there's something. I'm going back to see."

Whereupon, she slid down from the saddle, knotted her reins around a sapling, and ran back the way she had come. The old man just sat his horse, looking puzzled, but Stalwart was right on her heels.

"What sort of something?"

"Magic, of course. I don't know what. Not a sort I've ever met before."

Night was falling. Seen from this side, the

path they had followed down the great step was barely visible in the shrubbery. It showed as a narrow ledge around the side of the Hole, and then disappeared into that jumble of rocks between the base of the cliff and the plunging rapids. It was hard to know exactly where Emerald had stopped. But there *was* something there, pinned under a shadowed overhang, half in and half out of the torrent.

Hoping for a better view, Stalwart stepped onto a flattish boulder in the stream. He jumped to another beyond it . . . and another . . . then a larger one, a tiny island in midstream with water rushing by on both sides. Emerald followed him, tried to join him, and missed her footing. He grabbed; she grabbed. They teetered in mortal peril for a long and horrible moment before regaining their balance. He swallowed his heart back down where it belonged.

She put her mouth to his ear and yelled, "Thanks!"

He wanted to make a joking response and couldn't think of one, so he pointed instead. Now they had a clear view, except that spray kept blowing in their eyes.

"It's a body!" she shouted.

He nodded. It might well be a body. If it was a body, he was most utterly, completely, positively sure that it was a *dead* body. He was going to be very surprised if it was not the missing Rhys. To let the old man see his grandson in that position would be horribly unkind. Common sense said to say nothing more, go back to Waterby, and return with a team in the morning. On the other hand, if the water rose in the night, the river would take that corpse away, never to be seen again. Had Emerald not sensed the magic, they would have missed it altogether. Why should there be magic associated with a corpse?

He recalled that Mervyn had a coil of rope hung on his saddle.

On horseback, the old forester had seemed younger than his years. Back on ground level, he was again tiny, frail, and stooped. There was not a thing wrong with his wits, though. His bleak expression showed that he had guessed what they had seen.

"I think it may be a body, grandfather," Stalwart said. "We can't get it out, but if we had some rope we could tether it so it won't wash away."

The old man turned to his horse. "No forester ever goes anywhere without a bit o' rope, lad."

That was a pity. Someone was going to have to do some death-defying acrobatics, and Stalwart knew who that someone was. He was a skilled juggler and tumbler, but he had never performed on the lip of a giant sewer before.

He told Emerald, "It'll be dark by the time I'm finished. So you may as well go back up that cliff before the light goes. I don't intend to disappear into that pit, but if I do, one of us must get back to report. And I'll be beyond help. So no dramatic rescues! You go back to Waterby and wait for Snake. Understood?"

She gave him a hard stare. "Yes, Sir Stalwart."

He distrusted her when she called him that. "Promise?"

"Didn't you just give me an order, *sir*?"

"Yes."

"Then why do you need to ask me for a promise?"

He was never going to understand girls.

He gave her his sword and commission for safekeeping. He stowed his cloak, hat, and jerkin on Snowbird and handed the reins to Mervyn. When the horses set off back down the trail, he followed on foot with the rope slung over his shoulder. He watched them pass safely around the edge of the Hole and start the climb up the big step. As he drew close to the falls, the roar of the waters grew ever more menacing. He was aware of being frightened, and that made him angry. To delay would be cowardice. *Get on with it!*

He clambered along the water-slick rocks to what he thought must be about the right place. Back in his soprano year in Ironhall, he had learned some good knots from Sailor, who had been Prime then—a lesson in knots in exchange for a lesson in juggling. Sailor had died on the Night of Dogs, last Firstmoon, battling monsters in the King's bedchamber.

For this job, Stalwart needed nothing fancy. A clove hitch was enough to fasten one end around a well-wedged tree trunk. He used a simple bowline to fashion a noose and fitted it loosely around himself under his arms. That might stop him being swept over the falls if he slipped. A running bowline would pull tight and hold more firmly, but might also cut him in half if he was trapped in the full force of the torrent. More likely the river would smash him to a jelly first. Already spray had soaked through his hose and doublet and his hands were aching with the cold; there was so much noise he couldn't hear his teeth chattering.

He started down the rock pile. It was not a

long climb, no more than the height of a cottage, and the river offered him a convenient ladder—a tree lodged almost vertically inside a smooth circular chimney that the falls had carved out of bedrock. It had not been in the river long enough to lose all its branches, and the stubs stuck out like rungs. All in all, it seemed so handy that he wondered if it could be some fiendish trap. It worked, though. He made his way almost to water level without trouble, but there his view was blocked by the sides of the chimney.

With silent thanks to the memory of Sailor and that knot lesson, he bent the line around the tree and secured it. Then he let the noose take his weight while he braced his feet against the trunk and leaned outward. He ended almost horizontal, with his head practically at water level. Downstream there was nothing except a ghastly, shiny-smooth black slide down . . . down . . . down. . . .

Shuddering, he turned to look upstream. There was the body, just out of reach, and higher than he was. It had been swept in under the overhang and run aground on a sloping rock, but most of it was still underwater. It looked very precarious, ready to cast off at any minute. Its feet were toward him, and the legs were moving in the current, as if Rhys were marching, marching, marching to the country of the dead. That it was Rhys there could be no doubt. What was left of the clothing was visibly a forester's green, even in that gloom.

Meanwhile, Stalwart was soaked and exhausted and a long way from home. Also a long way from that corpse he had come to save. He hauled himself upright with rapidly numbing hands. He untied the rope from the tree and started climbing. The rope kept snagging, of course, and delaying him.

He really ought to leave Rhys where he was. The man's spirit had already returned to the elements, and the underground river might dispose of his corpse even faster than a proper funeral pyre would. It was wrong to risk a live man for a dead one. But the body was important evidence against the Fellowship of traitors. Also there was old Mervyn, who had been helpful. There were Rhys's wife and three children . . .

Reaching the top of his rope, Stalwart crouched for a moment on his hands and knees, catching his breath. Then he secured the rope to a boulder, a few steps farther upstream. He paused to plan what he would do. Even if he could get close to the body—and he had no great confidence that he could—he was certainly not going to crawl in under the overhang. It was lying with its head upstream. . . . He would have to try to lasso it with a hangman's noose. A gruesome way to treat a corpse, yes, but he had no other means to secure it by himself in near darkness. He tied a slip knot, put the loop around his upper arm so he would not lose it, and started down the cliff again, this time working his way spiderlike, with his face to the rocks.

A savage tug at his right boot warned him that he had put it in the river. He returned that foot to its previous position and then clung there, sprawled on a rock face, not quite vertical and very insecurely attached. An adjacent boulder was flattish and stuck out over the water—he was almost certain that it was the one pinning poor Rhys. Of the body itself, however, there was no sign.

Inch by inch, Stalwart transferred himself to the ledge, which was just barely wide enough for him to stand on. Once he was on it, he then had to lie down. Having achieved that, gripping tight to the rope with one hand and the rock with the other, he wriggled forward and hung over the edge to peer in under the overhang. He found himself staring into two lifeless eyes just above water level.

It wasn't Rhys after all. It was Lord Digby. Stalwart was so startled that he almost let go of the cliff.

13

Homecoming

The horse they had given Badger was a mean, ugly piebald whose high, hard trot made him ride like a sack of rocks. Badger barely noticed. His mind was roiled by the staggering realization that *now he did not have to die!* Eventually, yes. Of course. Everyone must die, but for most people it was a distant prospect, something that need not happen for fifty years. Facing certain death in a month or two changed life considerably.

Beset by his thoughts, he reached the ford over the Swallowbeck long before he expected it. He reined in Sack-of-rocks and sat for a moment, debating. Fortunately the Buran road here was a mere track through trees and presently deserted, so no one observed the young traveler's strange indecision. This was his moment of choice, the turning point of his life. Why had that young pest given him the jeweled star? The decision would have been easy without Wart's unwelcome display of trust.

If Badger carried on to Buran he would catch the evening ferry, then do as the uppity kid had ordered—ride to Grandon and the court, tell Snake what had happened. And the next time Ambrose came to Ironhall, Badger would die.

The alternative was to head up the Swallowbeck, the road to Smealey Hole. Then he would not have to die, because there, too, he would deliver news: news that the Fellowship was suspected of murdering Lord Digby and conspiring to assassinate the King; news that there was a White Sister in the area, sniffing out magic, and also a swordsman of the Royal Guard—even if he did stand shoulder high and still had his milk teeth. *Not fair!* whispered his conscience. *Stalwart is not as young as that. In a fair fight, rapier against saber, he would beat you every time.*

If he went home to Smealey, Badger might not die.

Home?

Yes, home. To see his home again, even if it must be for the last time . . . With a groan, Badger turned his horse's head to the north and set off up the Swallowbeck.

* * *

Few people would have noticed that road. The streambed itself was the path, a winding course of shingle holding a few small ponds. In the spring the stream was more evident, but rarely fierce enough to bother a horse. Pebbles crunched under his mount's hooves.

The cards were dealt, the decision made. He was *not* going to die in the Forge at Ironhall! As wild relief surged through him, he rose in his stirrups, waved his hat in the air, and let out a long howl of triumph. *He would live!* Sack-of-rocks whinnied in terror at this madness and broke into a gallop. Badger gave him his head and went racing along the Swallowbeck, screaming with joy.

All too soon he had to regain control and soothe the stupid animal, for he came to the second turning. The Smealey road branched off, becoming an obvious man-made track through the trees. It seemed smaller and meaner than he remembered, though, more overgrown. It climbed steeply to cross Chestnut Ridge, then plunged down into the valley of the Smealey.

Only now did he consider the possibility that Owen might not be there. Owen might very well be somewhere in or near Grandon, preparing to strike down King Ambrose as he had struck down Lord Digby. Never for a moment since Wart had told him of the murder and the connection to Smealey Hall had Badger doubted that the Fellowship was guilty, or that Ambrose was its true quarry. Digby, he assumed, had seen or heard something that had tipped the Fellowship's hand. They had perhaps been forced to strike before they were completely ready. The Blades kept nattering about the Monster War, but the Monster War was less than a year old. Owen's campaign went back a lot further than that. Owen's implacable purpose had always been to kill the Chivian tyrant.

But if Owen wasn't *here*, right *now,* then things might become complicated.

No matter, he had made his decision. . . .

Halfway down the slope, the trail went by the ruins of a massive beech tree, perhaps a hundred years dead. Long ago it had rotted, or been struck by a lightning bolt and burned. All that was left was a huge columnar stump about three man-heights high. It was also hollow, although the opening was not visible from the trail.

Badger reined in with his sight blurred by tears and a lump in his throat big enough to choke him. He remembered the day Lloyd and Kendrick had decided to turn the hollow tree into a castle and had lit a fire in it to clean out the ants and make it bigger. They had come so close to setting the whole forest ablaze that the Baron had whipped them till they howled, sending little Bevan into a fit of screaming terror. Then there was the day little Bevan, grown old enough to apply the family talent for devilry, had hidden in that tree until the entire population of Smealey had been turned out to beat the woods in search of him. Memories—much later memories—of leaving food there to feed an outlaw Ceri . . .

He dismounted and led Sack-of-rocks over to the verge. The hollow tree would still be an excellent hiding place. Its wormy, dirty interior looked as if no one had been there since the last time he had peered in and found a pathetic cache of Ceri's personal treasures: his pouch, his sword, his hunting horn, his dagger. Ceri had left them there on the day he rode off to Waterby to die, knowing that Bevan would find them. Ceri, twelve years dead. *Vengeance is coming soon now, Ceri. One way or the other, you will be avenged. You and the others . . .*

To ride into Smealey Hole today wearing a cat's-eye sword might be fast suicide. Badger laid *Durance* in the tree; it could endure there until he returned for it. If Owen sent him back, he would retrieve it on the way out. If not—if he was to live—then an Ironhall sword was worth a fortune anywhere outside the country; only in Chivial were cat's-eyes reserved to the King's Blades.

He swung himself up into the saddle and urged Sack-of-rocks into a canter. The sun was very close to setting as he forded the river. Memories came thick as midges at twilight now . . . the meadow where Kendrick taught him to ride, where Aneirin taught him to shoot a longbow . . . the hayloft where young Bevan hid to watch Lloyd kissing the plowman's daughter . . . the still pools of the Smealey, where the Baron went fishing.

The valley was a bowl enclosed by a rampart of rock, lowest on the west. Its bottomland had long since been stripped of trees, but it had never been fertile enough to farm. The Smealeys had grazed cattle there. Evidently the Fellowship of Wisdom did not, probably because herds needed herders, who would be unnecessary witnesses to things better left unseen. Bracken, saplings, and man-high thistles had taken over the pasture. The river snaked across the plain in a steep-sided channel, plunged along a canyon cutting through that low western side, then vanished into a bottomless pit.

Smealey Hall stood on a flat-topped knoll.

On two sides the ground dropped almost sheer to the treacherous river; to north and east it sloped gently. Some of the mismatched cluster of buildings had been built by Baron Modred or his father, others were centuries old. It was not a castle, because fortification required royal permission to crenulate and King Ambrose would not grant that to Smealey Hole in the next ten thousand years. A site so defensible must have been a fortress many times in the past, though. Traces of ancient walls could still be found in the turf.

No dogs barked as the stranger rode up the trail, which was another change from the old days. No guards challenged, but Badger was certain his arrival would have been noted. Thoughts of archers waiting with strung bows made the back of his neck prickle as he rode across the flat summit to the residence door. He could hear chanting coming from somewhere, voices taking turns at evoking spirits, in the way of conjuration everywhere.

There was not as much as a cat in sight when he halted Sack-of-rocks beside the steps. He swung his leg over the saddle, dropped down, turned, and found himself facing three grim swordsmen. He could almost believe they had used magic to make that dramatic arrival, except that magic was too valuable to waste on party tricks.

They were not wearing armor. Even this backwood scholastic retreat must receive visitors sometimes, and the Privy Council would jump cloud high if it heard rumors of a private army in Nythia. So they bore no visible steel except their swords and daggers, but their jerkins and britches were of stout leather, padded to deflect all but the heaviest or most skillful strokes. There might be metal under their floppy plumed hats. If he had kept *Durance* with him, he could have demonstrated what an Ironhall man thought of three scowling yokels. But then four more came strolling around the corner of the house to take up position in the outfield. Even an Ironhall man must shun those odds.

"Identify yourself," growled the one wearing a sergeant's red sash. He was big, powerful. His face was a hideous ruin, an untidy wad of hair and twisted leather, decorated with old scar tissue. One eye was a gaping hole and half his nose had gone. He looked as if he had been used for broadsword practice by all the Ironhall fuzzies at once.

"I am a friend of Brother Owen."

"No brother here by that name."

"Have I misjudged his title? Have you another Owen?"

"None."

Owen might be using another name or the man might be lying.

"Identify yourself," the sergeant repeated, laying a hand on his sword hilt.

Badger cursed his folly in coming unarmed. He could not hope to fight so many, but they would not bully him like this if he bore a sword. The distant chanting had ended, he noticed.

"My name is my business," he said stubbornly. "Go to Owen and describe me." He removed his hat.

He had worried that Owen might have started losing his hair now, but it was clear at once that the gamble had paid off. All three jaws dropped.

The Sergeant recovered first, a sneer pulling up his scarred lip to display wide gaps in his teeth. "If you're not who I think you are, sonny, I'll rearrange you until you look worse than I do."

"I am."

The man grunted. "Gavin, run and tell the Prior his brother's here to see him."

14

Reunion

The youngster called Gavin ran—not into the residence, but across the yard to the elementary. The sergeant gestured for Badger to follow and then walked just behind him, within striking distance. He was being extraordinarily cautious, but that was a strong hint that Owen was in charge. Owen never left anything to chance.

The elementary was the oldest building on the site, dating from dark ages long ago. Originally it must have been a warriors' feasting hall, but Badger could recall it being used for that purpose only once. In some more recent time, an octogram had been inset in the floor to turn it into an elementary. Serious sickness or injury had been treated there by healers summoned from Waterby. Most of the time it had just stood empty, a marvelous haunt for bats, rats, and small boys.

The man who emerged just as Badger

reached the steps was clad in the floor-length gown of a sorcerer, black in his case. The cord around his waist was gold, which was usually the mark of a prior. He halted and stared down at the visitor, then reached up and threw back his hood to reveal a face very similar—rugged rather than handsome, stubborn, distrustful, wearing at the moment a wry, slightly lopsided smile. His dark hair was blazoned with a silver streak.

"Owen!"

"Bevan!"

They met in a rib-cracking embrace halfway up the steps and pummeled each other in the delight of reunion. It had been four years since they'd parted at the doors of Ironhall.

They went inside with their arms around each other, babbling the nonsense that is evoked on such occasions: "By the spirits, you're not the boy I remember." "You haven't changed a bit." "It's been a lifetime!" . . . The joy became unbearable, Badger-Bevan's eyes flooded and his voice cracked.

Owen released him abruptly, mood changing like a whip crack. "What's wrong? *Why are you here?"* He had never approved of unmanly displays of emotion, even from a small boy. Tears had always provoked him to harsher punishment.

Badger drew one shuddering, deep breath and had himself under control again. "Sorry. My . . . seeing you . . . home . . ."

The elementary had been built entirely of vertical oak timbers, from an uneven stone floor to a too-high roof, whose rafters were home to bats and birds. It could never have been a comfortable place. Smoke would have filled it whenever the open hearth was lit, and the windows admitted little light, being mere slots through the massive walls. The small room at the back had perhaps been the master's sleeping quarters, but it had been a later addition, of inferior timber. The minstrel gallery along one side was probably even more recent, but it listed badly.

The Fellowship had made some effort to clean it up. The eight-pointed star of the octogram was more obvious. Walls, which had no doubt once borne displays of weapons, battle honors, and hunting trophies, were now hung with cabalistic inscriptions on long scrolls. Since a lesson had just ended, the novices in their white gowns stood clustered around adepts, hearing of their failings and successes. They all had their hoods up, so only varying heights suggested which were men and which women—black and white, like pieces in some gigantic board game.

Yes, Owen had wrought changes, but bring back a roasting ox and a hundred drunken warriors swilling mead and the elementary would again be barbarically impressive. Badger had seen it like that once, the night Ceri raised the banner of rebellion, proclaiming Nythian independence to the cheers of his patriot zealots. Ceri was twelve years dead and the child who had hidden up in that minstrel gallery that momentous night was a grown man now. Yet he felt himself quail under Owen's terrible stare, and was amazed to discover that Owen could still terrify him. Owen was quite capable of sending him back to Ironhall to die.

"I came to warn you that you're under investigation. The Privy Council is after you."

"The Council? Not just the Old Blades?"

"The Council."

The Prior's eye gleamed. "Why?"

"For the murder of Lord Dig—"

"It worked?" Owen shouted. "He did die? How? How do you know?" He grabbed his brother's shoulders as if to crush them. Four years of scholarship had not weakened the demonic grip he had earned in a lifetime of weapons training.

Badger winced and squirmed loose. "You

don't know this? He dropped dead in the middle of a state reception, in full view of the entire court, practically at the King's toes."

Owen closed his eyes in ecstasy. "I did not know. We were still waiting to hear. And a court reception . . . We did not plan *that*! How wonderful are these tidings!"

"You did it from *here*? Across the whole width of Chivial?"

The Prior smiled like a well-fed wolf. "Oh, we have some greatly devious sorcerers in the Fellowship, believe me." Abruptly his mood changed again, and he impaled his brother with a dark and deadly stare. "But how do *you* know, mm? Ironhall hears the news and you leave your post?" They who plot treason must be ever on guard against treachery, and a naked sword would have been no greater threat than his suspicion. "Come and let us talk, brother!" he said softly.

"Of course, brother." *He is going to send me back,* Badger thought, and the terror rose again like fire in his throat.

The Prior's office in the residence had once been the Baron's office. Here, too, ancient clutter had been replaced by new. The brothers sat on opposite sides of a table heaped high with papers, while Badger told the story of how he came to be there, back home at Smealey Hole. Owen did not offer food and drink, as one should to a guest who has traveled far. He just sat, still as a corpse, staring at his brother as if watching the words emerge from his lips.

He will send me back! Badger had sworn an oath. He wondered if he would hold Owen to his word, were their positions reversed. They were very much alike, so alike that he had always assumed they shared the same mother. He did not know that and never could. Although the Baron had collected several luscious beauties during his life and flaunted each in turn as his wife, there had in fact been only one true Baroness. Anwen had been an extraordinary woman, tough as iron and ugly as a plowman's boot. Rumor, those terrible stories that sprouted like weeds around the House of Smealey, insisted that she had disposed of her rivals, one after another, by way of the river. She had certainly reared all of Modred's sons, but how many had been hers she had somehow kept a secret, even from them. Perhaps none, because none had looked in the least like her. They had all been handsome: Ceri, Aneirin, Edryd, Kendrick, Lloyd, and Owen. Then Bevan, nine years later. Owen and Bevan, the last two born, the last two still living, two too much alike.

Outside the tiny window, the light was fading fast. Only when Badger ended his story did Owen speak.

"So you have delivered your warning. What do you do now?"

With dry mouth, Badger said, "Whatever you wish. I can catch the morning ferry and ride to Grandon. If asked to explain the delay, I can claim my horse went lame. But the Old Blades will be here within two days, I promise you. Did you buy off the Sheriff of Waterby, or just frighten him away?"

Owen sneered contempt. "None of my doing. The cold shadow of death has shriveled his manhood." He clasped his thick hands, as he did when he was thinking. "Where do you stand in Ironhall?"

"I am Prime." There was the agony.

"Already?"

Four years ago he had sworn his oath. He would claim to be only fifteen, he had said. Get him enrolled, he had promised Owen, and he would work his heart out every day for the next five years. He would be one of the best. The best went into the Guard, bound by the King himself. Bevan Smealey had been no stranger to a sword, even then, although what Owen had been teaching him was Isilondian technique, quite different from Ironhall style; in some ways it had been a hindrance. But he had done well and won praise. Ironically, his success had hardly mattered. Every live body went into the Guard now, to make up the losses of the Monster War. He had been granted only four years, not five.

"Already. Leader told me they would have bound more of us last time except the Guard cannot strip Ironhall of all its seniors. They need us to coach the kids." Two months, no more, Bandit had said, and that had been two weeks ago. "But you, brother? What of *your* oath?"

Owen's eyes shone wolflike in the gloom. "Close, very close! I did what I promised, I collected the finest team of enchanters ever brought together. Digby was our final test. We have learned how to slay at a distance—any distance. If the tyrant flees to the ends of the earth, he cannot escape me!"

He is going to send me back. They had sworn to slay King Ambrose. They had shaken hands on it, that the oath would bind both until one succeeded. They had agreed that Owen would set up the school of magic he planned and Bevan would enroll in Ironhall. When King Ambrose tried to bind Candidate Badger, Badger would kill him, but then he must die as well, cut down by the Guard. No more than six weeks left—was it so surprising that he slept poorly now?

"How soon can you do this?" He was ashamed to hear a tremor in his voice. He did not want to die.

Owen sighed. "As soon as I can find the link I need, and that is a matter of chance. As when Digby came here last week. He recognized me—not me personally, but this." The Prior's fingers touched the silver streak in his hair. "Ceri and Kendrick had it also, remember? Anwen told me once that the Baron had it in his youth, but he lost his hair early. Digby was Ambrose's Master of Horse in the Nythia campaign. The day Lloyd and Kendrick and the others ambushed the King outside Waterby, he saw the bodies after Durendal had finished with them. He probably saw Ceri the following year when they cut his head off, if not before." Owen bared his teeth. "And then he saw this badge of ours again, right here in Smealey Hole. He knew the Privy Council would not rejoice to hear that a Smealey was running a school of magic in the traitors' nest."

"He wanted the Sheriff to bring his Yeomanry against you."

Owen shrugged. "I gambled that the decrepit

Florian would not heed his bluster."

"It's amazing he did not send a letter to Snake."

"He did send a letter. The boy taking it to the ferry was very happy to exchange it for a handful of gold. We used Lord Digby as a test of our new sorcery, and it worked. It worked!" He licked his lips. "Wonderful news!"

Struggling to seem calmer than he felt, Badger asked, "What is this link you need to slay Ambrose?" *And to free me from my oath.*

"A gift," his brother said. "The subject must be linked to another person by the giving or receiving of a gift. The link does not last long, as you may guess, just a few days. Like gratitude. We need the gift itself and the other person. Digby's guide here was a forester named Rhys. He gave him a gratuity, of course, as expected."

"A hunting horn. I heard of it. I don't understand how that—"

"It is just the way the sorcery works," Owen said dismissively. "It strengthens the spiritual link between them, making it so strong that when we kill one, the other dies also. We needed a few days to lure Rhys within our reach, but we got him, and the sorcery worked. I ran Rhys through with a sword myself, and you tell me that Digby fell dead in front of the King! Wonderful! But it may take a long time to locate someone linked that way to the tyrant, and then snare him while the link is still effective."

A wild surge of excitement made Badger stutter. "G-g-gift? Someone the King's given a gift to recently?"

Owen's eyes narrowed suspiciously. "A physical object, not just a title or a word of praise. And it must be freely given."

Badger chuckled. The chuckle became a snigger, then laughter. Tears came to his eyes as all his pent-up terror was released in helpless bellows of mirth.

"Stop it!" his brother roared, rising. "What's the matter with you! Pull yourself together!"

Badger pulled himself together. He gasped, choked, and then wiped his eyes. "I have exactly what you need, Prior Owen, and the man you want is undoubtedly snooping around the valley at this very moment. He was coming in by the canyon road. The King hung this on him just the night before last." He tossed out on the table a diamond-studded brooch in the form of a star.

15 Unwelcome Discovery

It was a small miracle that Sir Stalwart, companion in the Loyal and Ancient Order of the King's Blades, did not topple off the rock and perform a graceful seal dive into the black water racing right under his head. He hauled himself up with the aid of the rope and wriggled backward until more of him was supported. He felt giddy—from being upside down, or the shock, or both.

He had first seen Digby more than two years ago, droning on about honor and service on Durendal Night. He had seen him again in the palace. Although they had not been close on either occasion, he was absolutely certain that the man in the water was Digby—and Digby clad in the remains of a forester's green. This was madness! No one could have spirited that corpse from Grandon all the way here. And for what purpose? Just to flush it down Smealey Hole?

The body in the water must be the real Lord Digby, and the man who had died in Nocare had been an imposter. Just because no one had ever heard of an enchantment that would make one man look exactly like another did not mean that one could not be invented. The switch had been made when he'd visited Smealey Hall, and the phony had been sent back with Rhys. . . .

There were maggots in that theory. Why had none of Digby's retainers detected the change? Or the King, his friend? Why had the White Sisters not sensed the magic on him when he entered the hall . . . ? And the wrong man had died anyway! Why? How? Had the fake Lord Digby intended to kill the King and somehow turned the sorcery on himself? And why had the White Sisters not detected *that* piece of magic when he brought it in? Why had the imposter not made his move the previous evening, when he'd supped with the King?

Shivering on the rough slab with his head and shoulders still overhanging the river, Stalwart realized that no one would believe his story without evidence. He edged forward and downward again and took another look at the corpse. The only part of it that he could possibly hope to catch with a noose was the head, but that was resting on the rock below, with only the face out of water. It wouldn't work.

He had to try at least once. He stretched the noose wide, then lowered it into the water. The current swept it away, twirling the rope like a spinner's yarn. He hauled it in and tried again, this time casting it upstream in the hope it would have time to sink before it was washed down to the body. That worked no better. What he needed was a pole with a hook. Not having one, he must just come back in the morning with helpers and hope the body was still there.

Wearily he began to clamber up the rocks. Shock and disappointment lay on him like a wagonload of tiles. Two nights without—no, really *three* nights without enough sleep. Plus two long rides—Valglorious to Grandon, then Grandon to Waterby. He needed a soft, warm bed more than anything.

He reached the top, where he had tied the rope. He pulled his shoulders over the edge and was about to grab a handy branch of driftwood to pull himself farther when he realized that the branch was, in fact, one of a pair of boots. Emerald! He had given her strict orders not to come back to help.

Yelling over the roar of the falls: "I thought I told you—"

Those boots were far too large to be hers.

And there were more of them. Eight in all. Balanced on one foot and the toes of another, gripping rocks with bloody, frozen hands, he felt himself freeze in a rush of despair. He had failed.

He had left *Sleight* with Emerald.

But that hardly mattered, because a sword now advanced until its point was right between his eyes.

"You must be Wart," said an unfamiliar voice. "Do you want to die now or later?"

16 Meanwhile, His Sword

Emerald had ridden to the top of the cliff with Mervyn, but there she reined in. "I'm going to wait here for Wart—I mean Sir Stalwart. Do you want to go on?"

The old man chuckled. "No, er . . . Master Luke. My eyes aren't what they were, but I can find the path in the dark and doubt you could. Nor yon stripling Blade neither."

"You were right earlier, Master Mervyn, when you called me 'lass.' I'm no Luke." She had decided that she could trust him, unlike his enchanted master, the Sheriff.

He cackled. "Your legs are wrong shape for a boy's, miss, but very fine indeed for girl's."

"Um . . . thank you." That was the first time a man had ever told her that. Of course until yesterday she had never displayed them in hose. So what if he was two hundred years old? It was a start.

"'Course a forester's trained to see what he's looking at, unlike most folk."

"Er, yes. My real name is Sister Emerald."

He coughed an *oof!* of surprise. "My lady! I did not dream—"

"That's all right. You could not know. That was how I found that body. It has magic on it. I am sorry, Forester, but I greatly fear it will prove to be your grandson."

He sighed. "Aye." And there was silence.

She dismounted and sat on a rock to wait. The old forester hobbled the horses and removed their bridles so they could graze. He perched on another boulder and time seemed to freeze.

Night fell. Wart did not come. She could see nothing down in the canyon shadows where the angry waters roared. She kept telling herself that he was an air person, nimble as a squirrel when it came to climbing.

Mother Superior had called him, "dangerously overconfident."

At last she said, "He should be here by now."

"Reckon so, my lady."

"I greatly fear that treason and black magic both are plotted in Smealey Hole these days."

"Aye, milady. Evil is a common crop there."

"Outsiders must visit it sometimes, though? Tinkers who mend pots?" That had been Badger's suggestion and she still had a painful distrust of that dismal man.

"Not many. Milady, Sheriff told us to stay away from the Hole. Got no cause to vex the conjurers, he says. But if they're behind Rhys going missing, and if they harm yon boy, then I know the lads will rally to my horn. Dozen of us, an' I can find half as many again, given a day."

Another day would be far too late. If the intruder had been spotted and those mysterious swordsmen had gone to investigate, Wart might be dead already. She was horribly conscious of the awkward weight of his sword at her side and his commission with the royal seal tucked away in her jerkin. His only hope was to be taken in for questioning, and that would provide only a brief and highly unpleasant delay before the same watery ending. He carried nothing to prove that he was anything more than a common poacher. What happened to petty poachers in Smealey country, anyway? No court could summon evidence from the bottom of the Hole.

When the stars came out, she knew that she could not go back to Waterby without finding out what had happened to Wart.

"Forester, Sir Stalwart has been delayed."

"Aye, milady."

"Detained, likely."

"Aye, milady."

"That's a breach of the King's peace, because he's an officer of the Crown. Will you please go back to Waterby and bring a posse? I leave it up to you whether you tell the Sheriff or just round up a bunch of your friends. Meet me here at sunup. If I'm not here, then I have been detained also. Come and rescue us."

She expected fifteen minutes of argument, but the old man cackled approvingly.

"Aye, milady! That I will. You can count on Mervyn."

This instant agreement was a little disconcerting. Suddenly she had no more reason to delay. "Then please leave the other two horses here. Thank you."

"Spirits keep you—Master Luke!"

"And good chance to you, Mervyn Forester," she said, striding off down the hill with the cat's-eye sword swaying at her side.

17 Baron Smealey

"I asked you, Wart," said the mocking voice, "if you want to die now or later?"

"Later would be better." He was probably not audible over the din of the falls. That his captors knew his name was the worst news of all. Lord Florian or almost anyone in Waterby Castle might have betrayed him, but only Badger and Emerald knew him as Wart. Enlisting Badger had been entirely his own idea, not one approved by Snake. This disaster was all his own fault.

"Come up," the man yelled, removing his sword from the end of Stalwart's nose. "I was told not to maltreat you as long as you behave yourself. If you give any trouble, I am to thrash you within an inch of your life. Clear enough?"

"Very transparent." Stalwart hauled himself wearily up, boots scrabbling on the rocks. He made such hard work of it that powerful hands grabbed his arms and lifted him bodily, then steadied him as he staggered. He was looking at the laces of a leather jerkin.

"This un's not big enough, Sarge!" roared a new voice. "Ought to throw it back."

All four of them stood head and shoulders above Stalwart, and twice as wide. All were stoutly clad in padded leather, armed with swords and daggers.

"Hands behind you," the leader shouted in his ear. "I'm told you're a lot more dangerous than you look."

"Wouldn't be hard," yelled one of the others, and they all hooted.

Who was Stalwart to disagree, stumbling, bumbling idiot that he was? He submitted in silence as his wrists were bound, and then a few turns taken around his elbows as well. Were they seriously worried that he might snatch a man's sword from his scabbard? That they felt the need to take such precautions was a compliment to the Blades' reputation—no credit to him.

"Move!" the Sergeant shouted, and off they all went along the rocky ledge, skirting drift-wood and ankle-breaking gaps in the footing. Stalwart had trouble balancing, but his captors stayed close and steadied him.

It was only a week since the last time he'd

been led around like a performing bear with a noose around his neck. He really should try and break the habit. His captor then had been the odious Marshal Thrusk, whom he had joyfully obliterated soon after. Thrusk had gone so far as to tow Stalwart behind his horse and had never tied a knot that did not hurt; but these men were being surprisingly considerate, as if they really had been ordered not to damage him.

When they had climbed up out of the canyon into the wider valley, they came to more men waiting with horses. Stalwart was lifted into a saddle like a child. He ought to feel flattered that whoever was in charge of this had felt the need to send so many men for him. He should have been more modest when he described his Quagmarsh exploits to Badger.

He would not be bragging much about this mission.

The Hall seemed to be a cluster of buildings arrayed around a central yard. From the way the rooflines blotted out the stars, some were two stories high; a few poorly shuttered windows showed chinks of candlelight. Bats squeaked and flittered overhead, which was common enough around country dwellings, but no dogs barked or came to greet the visitors. That was curious.

More leather-clad swordsmen appeared with lanterns. The prisoner was lifted from his horse's back, then led by his tether down some steps, with a lantern behind making shadows dance ahead. He noted a door of timbers as thick as his fist, a flagstone floor, glimpses of solid masonry walls, but it was the chill and the cloying scent of recently harvested apples that told him he was in a root cellar. Onions and carrots hung in nets overhead. Stacked casks and barrels took up at least half the space, but in the area left empty stood a single wooden chair. On an upturned bucket beside it were a pitcher, a loaf, and some cheese. His mouth started to water, traitor that it was.

The Sergeant hung a lantern on a chain dangling from the ceiling. "You'll be needing a blanket. Or two. We wouldn't," he added wryly, "want you to die of cold."

Stalwart was wet to the skin and shuddering, lacking cloak and jerkin. "Be nice," he admitted humbly. He would not be too proud to eat that food, either. When the bonds fell from his hands, he shot a quick glance behind him. Two other men were blocking the doorway, forestalling any attempt to dodge past the Sergeant and make a break.

The man was even larger than he had seemed in the dark. His features had been so horribly mangled that they seemed barely human. His remaining eye looked the prisoner up and down curiously. Mostly down, naturally.

"You really a *Blade,* sonny?"

"Naw! Give me a sword and I'll show you how bad I am with it."

"What's your second wish?"

"Yes, I am a Blade. And I'm on His Majesty's business. What you're doing here is treason."

"Yes, lad. I know." He chuckled. "I enjoy it. I also need the money, because I'll have to be very, very rich to find me a wife at my age. Don't bother trying to escape. This place was built to keep mice out. It can keep one dagger-sized Blade in. I'll send a man with the blankets. No, I'll send three men with the blankets, just so you won't be tempted."

He left, his subordinates backing away before him. The door shut with a squeal and a boom, followed by muffled sounds of bolts and bars rattling and thumping. By that time Stalwart was eating.

He had barely taken the edge of his hunger when the same racket recurred in reverse order, ending when the door squeaked open. A man entered and the whole performance was repeated. Someone was fanatically determined that the prisoner not escape.

That someone was almost certainly the man who was now locked in with him, for his sorcerer's cowled gown of midnight black was bound by the golden cord of a prior. He stood under the lantern so that his face was shadowed. Stalwart could make out only a square, clean-shaven chin and two dark, deep-set eyes.

"The King sends children against me!"

Stalwart leaned back, crossed his ankles, and continued to chew. "Traitors deserve nothing better."

"I am no traitor, for he was never my king! Look! I will demonstrate a little magic for you." From his sleeve the conjurer produced a horseshoe, seemingly a perfectly ordinary iron horseshoe, large enough to fit a cart horse or a knight's destrier. "Watch!"

He had very large hands, and his gown was stretched over an enormous chest and shoulders. Grunting with effort, he slowly wrenched the arms of the shoe apart. He did not quite straighten it, but he opened it to a crescent. This was a legendary test of strength that Master Armorer at Ironhall always declined to try, although he could sometimes be persuaded to lift anvils. To complete his act, the Prior threw the shoe on the flagstones, making it ring convincingly.

"Ta-rah!" Stalwart clapped his hands slowly. As a former gleeman, he could appreciate a good routine. But why bother performing for him?

A fine set of teeth flashed angrily in the shadow of the hood. "I wished to show you the wisdom of obeying my commands. Give me trouble, and I will break your arms with my bare hands. I can make you suffer unbelievable torments. Indeed, I intend to, but I prefer not to start just yet. It might lower your resistance."

Stalwart was locked in with a raving maniac, and the stench of madness made his scalp prickle. He shrugged. "You enjoy making others suffer?"

"No. It is because I have seen so much suffering that I intend to punish the criminal responsible. I understand that you claim to be a Blade, and yet you have never been bound."

"Yes."

"Show me."

Stalwart rose uneasily and unlaced his doublet, then opened his shirt to show that he bore no binding scar over his heart. "Satisfied?"

"Yes. A major conjuration like that would

interfere with the enchantment I have planned for you."

As he dressed again, Stalwart recalled the late and unlamented Marshal Thrusk. He, too, had checked his prisoner for a binding scar, and would have slain him instantly had he found one. Now the situation was apparently reversed: it was the absence of one that had landed him in trouble this time.

"So when does the show begin?" The cellar was icy. He was trying as hard as he could not to shiver, lest this demented sorcerer think he was afraid. In fact, of course, he was absolutely terrified. Fortunately threats always raised his dander and made him smart-alecky.

"As soon as the novices have been sent off to bed. Where are the woman and the old forester?"

"When I found the body, I sent them for help." Oh, flames! He should not have mentioned the body. There went the evidence! To hide his dismay, he sat down and tore another hunk off the loaf with his teeth.

The Prior chuckled. "I guessed that was what you were doing in the rapids with a rope. I shall see that the corpse is properly disposed of as soon as there is light. Your remains may even make it down the Hole before his do, but I hope you will last longer than that."

What sort of man gloated over a helpless captive like this? It was a serious defect of character and there ought to be some way to exploit it. His identity was an easy guess.

"I assume your spite against me is because I am a Blade? You will take revenge on me because Sir Durendal slew two of your brothers?"

"I had not thought of that. Now you mention it, it will add to my pleasure."

"You are Badger's last remaining brother, of course?"

"His name is Bevan!" The sorcerer threw back his hood. The family resemblance would have been noticeable even without the white lock above the forehead. In his case it showed more as a streak than a tuft, because his hair was not curly. "I am Owen, fourth Baron Smealey."

"No you're not." Stalwart spoke with his mouth full, waving a chunk of cheese in one hand and an onion in the other. "When—which one was it? I lost count. When another of your awful brothers strangled your old man, Ceri was still alive. He would have inherited the title. Then he was convicted of treason, so all his lands and goods were forfeit and the title revoked. There is no Baron Smealey."

The Prior lunged forward, grabbed him by the front of his doublet and lifted him one-handed. Stalwart forced himself to keep still and just hang there, feet dangling, although he was choking as the mighty fist pressed up under his chin.

"But I am still rightful Prince of Nythia, aren't I? Say it: Yes, Your Highness!"

With all the breath he had left, Stalwart let him have the whole mouthful—cheese, onion, and a great spray of spit.

The Prior roared in revulsion and threw him away. Stalwart struck the chair, rolled off sideways, and bounced to his feet, grabbing the water pitcher to use as a weapon. He had acted without weighing the cost, and he realized now that it might be very high indeed.

But the madman did not leap at him. He wiped his face on his sleeve and laughed. "You will pay for that, runt—pay and pay! You swore to die for your tyrant king. Well, tonight you will die for him, I promise. Over and over, hour after hour!"

Wheeling around, the madman beat on the door with his fist, and the guards outside began clattering locks and bolts again to open it.

Had the rest of the awful brood been as bad as this one? Or had some been more like

Badger, who was decent enough under his surly manner? Owen was obviously madder than a bated bear. Why had Badger come home to aid his hopeless cause?

18 Sir Emerald

Before she was halfway down the precipice, Emerald realized that her madcap rescue effort was unwise, but carrying on already seemed easier than turning back. The sword had taken on a fiendish, spiteful life of its own. It stuck out in front and behind, tangled in the undergrowth, and not infrequently managed to find its way between her knees. Now she understood why Wart had discarded it before going after the body in the river, and why the seniors at Ironhall were allowed a year's practice in wearing the accursed things.

By the time she was three-quarters of the way down, the light had failed completely and she was calling herself every kind of raving lunatic. She slithered and slipped and stumbled, no longer sure she was even on the trail and very much aware of the roaring waterfall below her. What could she really hope to accomplish by setting herself up as a knight errant? The chances that she might manage to return Wart's sword to him in a situation where he could use it were closer to invisible than the feathers on an egg. And reading out his commission to impress a gang of murderers did not seem a very promising program either.

She could not believe that Wart had been so clumsy as to fall in the river, but there was no sign of him on the path. Bruised, exhausted, and filthy, she came at last to the wide valley beyond the canyon, and the river of stars overhead spread out as a sea. There she could at least walk upright instead of scrambling along on all fours. Soaked by spray and too cold to stop, she had no other purpose than to continue her trek in search of Smealey Hall. She soon lost the trail, but if she stayed close to the riverbank—and not close enough to fall in—she must inevitably come to the little hill she had seen earlier. She set off through the rocks and weeds, waving the rapier in front of her like a blind person's cane.

An isolated dwelling on the edge of Brakwood would certainly have dogs, but the wind was toward her, so her scent ought to escape their notice for a while yet. She struggled through thistles and brambles, with every new step a chance to sprain an ankle. Eventually a toothy black shape rose ahead of her, cutting off the stars to become the roofline of the buildings she sought. Soon she could even see pale gleams of candlelight in windows and a puzzling flicker of firelight at ground level.

Bats squeaked and wheeled overhead. She heard a horse whinny. She stopped. Horses reminded her of dogs. One bark and she would be lost—or found, rather—with nowhere to run, men coming to see what the trouble was. . . . She could not imagine herself fighting off a pack of mastiffs with a rapier, although she would probably try if the need arose.

The fire was certainly a bonfire. Why would anyone waste valuable fuel outdoors at night? The smoke was drifting toward her, so the dogs should not scent her yet. Unable to think of anything better to do, she decided to risk going halfway up the slope in the hope that she might find out something—*anything*—useful.

Five or six steps later, she scented magic. Very faint. Very subtle, too. A peppery smell, was it? Or a gentle humming? Hard to say. She had been shown something like it in Oakendown, as an example of . . . of . . . of what?

She stepped a little closer. To her right? Closer yet? Ah! It was a warding. Not identical to the classroom example but very similar. There was a hint of death in it, too weak for it to be a physical threat. Most of it was air and fire, the elements of motion. If she went too close, it would set off an alarm somewhere. Any moving body would trigger it, including a dog's, so there would be no dogs here. It would be a very local spell, probably imprinted on a rock or a post, but there would be others, forming an enchanted fence all around the complex. Only a White Sister would even know the barrier was there.

Only a White Sister could hope to find a way past it!

To her right was the river. She set off to her left around the hill, staying at the very limit of her ability to sense the conjuration. As she expected, her path curved in toward the buildings until she sensed another source ahead of her. She proceeded in a series of arcs, skirting each ward in turn. That there would be a gap somewhere she did not doubt. The conjurations would weaken with time and have to be replaced often. In a sorcery school like this, that would certainly be a task for the novices. They would enchant the posts, or stones, or whatever it was they used, inside their octogram, then bring them out to repair the barrier. But the only way they could test their work would be to set off the alarms deliberately. Almost certainly they would have missed a spot or two.

They had. A stone wall could not stop magic altogether, but it would weaken an air spell, and she found a stub of an old stone wall. It had perhaps been an ancient fortification, because there was a ditch alongside it. In that, down at ground level, the warding was negligible. Slithering on her belly, Sister Emerald made a secret but extremely undignified entry into the compound of Smealey Hole.

A dozen or more buildings were grouped about a central yard. She had come a long way from the bonfire she had been tracking, so she skulked back around the dark perimeter toward it. The high building with lighted windows must be the main house, probably where the adepts lived. Her ears soon tracked voices to a couple of long sheds with many illuminated windows—she decided those were bunkhouses for servants or novices. Her nose identified the stable, brewhouse, chicken coop, bakery. But she also detected a nasty stench of magic as she went by a large, high building, which must therefore be the elementary.

She paused at the corner of a hay shed to inspect the bonfire that had guided her in. The three men sitting around it were serving no purpose she could think of unless they were guards, and the thing they were guarding was a low slate roof. The building itself must be mostly underground, either an ice house or a root cellar. The realization that Wart was still alive gave her a great rush of relief that made all the pain and fear and effort of the last few hours seem worthwhile.

Now, how could she get him out?

Behind the shed was a high tangle of weeds. Dropping to hands and knees again, she began to crawl. Unfortunately, the brush included a fair share of thorns, thistles, and sharp stones. Fortunately, the stinging nettles were past their stinging stage. Every few minutes she raised her head to look around, but the men were engrossed in a dice game, unaware of the curious local wind disturbing the vegetation. She had almost reached the building when she heard new voices, two men approaching from the main house. They were heading for the fire, though, and did not seem to have noticed her at all. If the prisoner was about to be moved elsewhere, she had arrived too late, but perhaps she could manage to throw him his sword while he was out in the open. She had seen Wart in action and knew how deadly he was.

Voices, mocking and resentful . . . a snarly order . . . then a clattering of bolts and bars. Emerald slithered faster, confident that the newcomers were making too much noise themselves to hear the rustles and crackles of her progress. Puffing, she reached the back of the roof just as the door was slammed shut again.

Through a small grille set in the stonework, she heard Wart's voice, and then Badger's.

19

The Seventh Brother

Since Owen's departure, Stalwart had been curled up on a sack of goose feathers—which was unfortunately the only one of its kind in the root cellar. He had built himself a cave out of apple barrels and boxes of sun-dried plums. In this lair he huddled around the lantern, hungry for any trace of warmth. The blankets he had been promised had not appeared. When he tried shouting through the door, the guards outside either did not hear or would not heed. If he put an ear to the jamb he could hear them out there, cursing over their dice, so he knew they had not gone away.

His stocktaking of his cell had not taken long. Although the building was old, it was solidly built of fieldstone and massive timbers, and he found no weaknesses he could use. The absence of mouse droppings proved that the roof was sound and the door was snug in its frame. There was no window, the only ventilation came through a shaft in the masonry of the rear wall, and that was barely wide enough to admit his arm. He reached in past his elbow before his fingers found a mesh of metal wire covering it on the outside. If he lit a fire to keep warm, he would suffocate.

He brooded on failure, which had an unfamiliar taste. Quagmarsh had been such a triumph! Now he had hatched a total calamity, and all because he had put too much trust in an old friend and not enough in a new one. Badger's horrified reaction to the first mention of Smealey Hole should have been a giveaway. So should his denial of his previous story that he had found a secret passage there. So should his announcement in Waterby Castle, shouted for the Fellowship's spies to hear. He had claimed to be unfamiliar with the area and then identified landmarks. Unwilling to believe an Ironhall brother would betray him, Stalwart had ignored Emerald's warnings.

Idiot! Sucker! As punishment for his stupidity, the youngest-ever Blade was going to have the shortest-ever career with the Guard. Alas, *Sleight* would never hang in the sky of swords at Ironhall, and the name of her owner would not be inscribed in the *Litany of Heroes*. He would vanish unheralded down the Hole, after whatever horrors the sorcerers had in store for him. Perhaps, as a last request, he would ask the traitors to explain how Lord Digby had managed to die twice.

The usual clattering of bolts and locks warned him of visitors. By the time they entered, the lantern was back on its chain and the prisoner was seated on the chair with his arms folded and ankles crossed, desperately trying not to shiver, although he was sure his lips must be blue. The first man in was Badger, wearing a sorcerer's black gown. On his heels came the big, hideous-faced sergeant, carrying a bundle. "Brought you some dry clothes," he said.

The door was being closed and barred again as usual. Neither man was armed; the soldier's scabbard dangled empty at his side. Prior Owen took precautions to lunatic extremes.

Stalwart had never wanted anything as he wanted those dry clothes. Perversely, therefore, he made no move when the Sergeant dropped the heap at his feet.

"What's the price?"

"No price," the ugly man growled. "You got splat-all to pay with."

Taking his time, Stalwart began unlacing his

doublet. "It took you long enough."

"Been busy."

"Sergeant Eilir has been working on your behalf," Badger said.

Stalwart stopped for a moment to stare at him. "I used to have a friend who looked just like you."

"You still do. I can't save your life, but I've arranged so you'll die quickly."

Wart peeled off his doublet. His fingers were almost too numb to manage shirt buttons. "You have curious ideas of friendship."

"I've been arguing for the last hour with a dozen sorcerers and a score of men-at-arms. It was only when Eilir backed me that Owen and his cronies yielded. They wanted to kill you by inches. Now he's agreed that he'll just cut your head off."

"Why?" Stalwart took up the clothes provided and discovered a hooded gown of black wool and a brown fur cloak, nothing else. He pulled on the gown. "It's murder. And treason. You can't expect to get away with this. What have I done?"

Badger sighed. He did look miserable, give him that. "You won that star from the King, that's what. The Fellowship has a spell that needs a link between the victim and someone else, and that link must be a gift. The star in your case—"

"And Digby gave Rhys a hunting horn?"

"Exactly. Did you get a good look at the body in the river?"

"It was—It *seemed* to be Digby."

Badger glanced at Eilir, who shrugged as if to say that revealing secrets to a man in Stalwart's position really could not matter.

"It wasn't him," the Sergeant growled. "It was the forester. The sorcery turns one man into a *simulacrum* of the other. By itself, the change is harmless and doesn't last long. The adepts practiced on one another and some of the novices, and they all changed back in a few days. But while the spell holds, whatever happens to the simulacrum happens to the original, or the other way round. Stick a pin in one and both will yell. Nobody knew if the effect went as far as causing death, so when they'd made the Digby simulacrum, Owen put a sword through his heart. He sent a man off to Grandon to find out what had happened, to see if the sorcery reached that far."

Stalwart stared in disbelief as he tried to comprehend this insanity. Trouble was, he *did* believe it. It was the implications. . . .

"Are you saying they're going to make me into a copy of King Ambrose? Me and what ox?

He's three times my size."

This time it was Badger who shrugged. "They say that size doesn't matter. I brought you the biggest robe I could find. And they're certain it doesn't hurt."

"Except when that mad brother of yours cuts off my head! I bet that stings." He dropped his britches and hose and wrapped himself up in the cloak, shivering more than ever.

"Yes!" Badger snapped. "We're going to cut Ambrose's head off just the way he cut off Ceri's and Aneirin's. You'll die by a sword, the way they did, and Kendrick and Edryd and Lloyd did! Owen and I are the only ones left, and we will have our revenge."

"The King's head will fall off while he's at breakfast?"

"Perhaps. He'll certainly die."

So would Stalwart. There were worse ways to die than having your head cut off. There were a lot more good ways to keep on living instead. "As I recall, Aneirin was executed for strangling your dad. I'm not saying your father didn't deserve it. I'm sure he did. But why wasn't Aneirin hanged like any other common killer?"

Eilir answered. "He asked to die beside his brother, and the King graciously granted his request."

Badger was scowling. "Listen, Wart. I'm sorry this has to happen, truly. I swore an oath . . ." He shot an uneasy glance at the Sergeant. "I was the baby, much younger than even Owen. I was only a child when Nythia rose against the tyrant. I worshiped my brothers—Ceri was the oldest, and the leader by right of perfection. There was nothing Ceri could not do, nothing he did not excel in. Everyone worshiped Ceri, so you can imagine how he seemed to me. And the rest were little behind him. Kendrick was a swordsman; Lloyd already a sorcerer of note, although only an amateur; Edryd an artist . . . But that doesn't do them justice. They were strong and skilled in a thousand ways and beautiful as the stars. They taught me everything. . . . Ceri rallied all Nythia and kindled the torch of freedom. Monster Ambrose brought in his army to stamp it out.

"By winter, half of my wonderful brothers were dead. Owen was at home, being passed off as just a boy, although he was fifteen and had seen some fighting near the end. Ceri and Aneirin were outlawed, hiding out in Brakwood. I was seven, old enough to help smuggle food to them. The wolves closed in. Sheriff Florian was sure that the fugitives were in the area; and he came here, to Smealey Hole, violating guarantees the

King had given the Baron. He took Owen and me away, and Anwen, our mother. He swore to the Baron that none of us would eat or drink until Ceri was turned over to him. Ceri surrendered, of course. He would have died for any one of us, let alone three." Badger fell silent.

No boy in Ironhall discussed his own past openly. Some of them had very lurid pasts and the others wanted everyone to think they did, too. So hints were allowed, but open bragging was cause for disbelief and retaliation. That way, everyone could pass as a murderer until proved guilty of innocence. Stalwart had never heard this terrible story; he did not want to hear it now. It was full of deceit and distortion, possibly direct lies, but it was also grievous and he did not want to feel sympathy for traitors.

"You're saying Aneirin was a little hasty when he strangled Daddy?"

"Aneirin was fine until the siege of Kirkwain. What he saw there unhinged him. He seemed to be recovered, but he had a brainstorm when he heard about Ceri. Owen wasn't there. Mother and I weren't strong enough to stop him."

"You *saw* it?" Stalwart squealed. "You were there?"

Badger chuckled, sounding not quite sane

himself. "Oh, we had exciting times in our family! When Aneirin realized what he'd done, he went to Waterby and asked to die in Ceri's stead. The King allowed them to die together. Kind of him, wasn't it? Understanding, you must agree?"

There was no answer to that.

"Tell him what happened next," Eilir said.

"After Father's death?" Badger was pale and his voice almost shrill, as the telling dug up memories he had buried long ago. "Ceri was the new baron. He had never sworn loyalty to the House of Ranulf, but he was found guilty of treason—the trial took all of half an hour. His life, title, and estates were forfeit. The very afternoon the news reached Waterby, the Sheriff came with his men and drove us out of the house in the clothes we had on our backs. Literally! Not even a cloak or hat. Yes, it was snowing." He stared defiantly at Stalwart, who said nothing.

"Owen, and Anwen, and me. Anwen's health was poor. She and I would certainly have died without Owen. He had just turned sixteen, but he kept us alive that winter. The next year he got us across the sea to Isilond. He hired on as a mercenary, and we all starved together on a man-at-arms's pay. For eight years he lived by the sword. Do you wonder that I love my brother, *Sir Wart*?"

Stalwart wasn't going to admit that. "He isn't worth spitting on, let alone loving! He doesn't trust you, Badger! How can you trust him? He sends this hired pikeman along with you and even disarms him. Did he think I'd grab the man's sword out of its scabbard? Or you would? Or we both would? He's crazy, raving, deranged!"

"He's careful," Eilir said, "the finest warrior I ever knew. No man ever outsmarts or outfights Owen Smealey. I hired him as a raw recruit and discovered he was already a match for half the men in the troop. Within a year he was my captain. I could tell tales . . ." He shrugged.

Stalwart ignored him and concentrated on the man he'd thought was his friend. "How did you end up in Ironhall? And why? You couldn't seriously have wanted to join the Guard."

Badger chuckled again, a sound to raise the hair on the back of a man's neck. "Owen made his fortune in loot eventually, but too late for Anwen. On her deathbed she made us both swear that we would be avenged on Ambrose of Chivial."

Stalwart shuddered. "Plague and corruption, man! Owen maybe. He was a mature, veteran soldier. But you? How old?"

"Sixteen."

"You were too young to—"

"Bah! How old are you now, Sir Wart?"

That was another question with no good answer. Not now. In a few more weeks the answer would be different. *There weren't going to be any more weeks!* There wasn't even going to be a tomorrow.

Badger sneered at the lack of response. "We came back to Chivial, Owen and I. He'd had enough of soldiering, and he'd conceived the idea of the Fellowship. The only real school of sorcery in Chivial was the College, and there were many sorts of enchantments it wouldn't teach that people wanted and would pay for. Owen, although no great enchanter himself, had the dream and the money and the leadership. The Crown had put Smealey Hole on the market; it would be an ideal location. And when he had built his team of sorcerers, he could move against the tyrant, as he had sworn. That left me. How does an eager young man go about assassinating a monarch guarded at all times by the finest swordsmen in the world?

He quirked an eyebrow. "No guesses? Need a hint? No man can bear arms in the King's presence, right?"

Stalwart said, "Oh, no!" but obviously the

answer was *Oh, yes!* In the ritual of binding, the Brat gave the candidate his sword; the candidate stood on the anvil to swear loyalty to the King, and then the King struck the sword through his heart to bind him. The same sword. The candidate had to pass that sword to the King. If he leaped down from the anvil and passed it point first, even the Blades present could never move fast enough to block him. "You're Prime!"

Badger's smile was right out of nightmare. "I hope that tonight you will relieve me of the need to go back, friend Wart." His eyes were too bright, his teeth too big. "But if I must go, I will go, because when Owen and I parted at the door of Ironhall, we swore to each other that we would not step off our chosen paths until Ambrose was dead. If I do go back, then the next binding he attempts will be his last. The sword will go through the *other* heart."

Stalwart was aghast. It was unthinkable. "All these years? All the time I have known you, you've been plotting this? But it's suicide! The Blades will kill you right away, and even if they don't, then you'll die a traitor's death." He shivered. They were all crazy, the whole Smealey brood. The curse on the Hole was plain insanity, nothing more. "No wonder Grand Master said you were jumpy! Fates, man! You put yourself under sentence of death?" He stared in horror at Badger's mocking smile. "All these years?"

"All these years. But now my good friend Wart has come along to save me at the last minute. It's you or me, Wart. More exactly, it's you for certain and possibly me as well, if tonight's attempt doesn't work. Tomorrow at dawn I carry on to Grandon with your message to Snake. If Owen has failed and the King lives, then I must return to Ironhall and the binding. They'll be starting very soon." He turned away.

"Wait!" Stalwart yelled, jumping up. "Badger, this is madness! It wasn't Ambrose who caused all the deaths and suffering, it was your precious Ceri! Nythia didn't rally to his banner, you know that. You heard the history lectures in Ironhall. Very few people supported him. Even your own father didn't!"

Badger kicked the door with his boot. Bolts and bars began clanking.

"He had no claim to the throne of Nythia!" Stalwart shouted. "The royal line died out ages ago. If anyone is heir to the old princes, it is Ambrose himself, through his great-umpteenth-great-grandmother. The people didn't want Ceri and his mad ambitions, nor his sinister friends, either."

Badger had his face to the planks, his back to

Stalwart, refusing to listen. Eilir was watching the argument with what might have been meant to be a smile.

"And you?" Stalwart yelled, turning on him. "Where does your loyalty come from? Just money? Friendship? Or are you as mad as the rest of them?"

"See this?" The Sergeant pointed to the nightmare ruin of his face. "I was about your age once, sonny. I looked human, those days. Quite good-looking, in fact." He took a step closer. "Not now, though! I lived in Waterby, see? I wasn't a soldier, not then. I was a glassblower's apprentice. Then the war came, and the siege." Another step made Stalwart recoil from the abhorrence leering closer. "Your precious Ambrose set his Destroyer General on us, hurling great rocks at the town. It was one of them hit a wall and exploded right in front of me." Another step, and Stalwart was back against the chair. "All the rest of my family died, so I was lucky, wasn't I?"

The door creaked. Stalwart ducked nimbly past the Sergeant and grabbed Badger as he tried to leave.

"Listen! Your darling Owen's unstable as a two-legged horse. Maybe he was a father to you, but he cared so little for you later that he made you swear to kill yourself. He wants to torture me to death! He's curdled in his wits. He's a raving, demented—"

Eilir's iron hand took him by the shoulder and hurled him back. His leg caught the chair and he pitched headlong. It was fortunate that he knew how to fall; perhaps even more fortunate that he was well padded by the thick gown and fur cloak. He didn't break anything. The door boomed shut behind the two men. Then came all the noisy rigmarole of shutting it.

Groaning, the prisoner sat up and rubbed his knee, his shoulder. His elbow hurt, too. He was starting to shiver again. Dead men didn't shiver.

A very soft whisper said, "Wart?"

20 A Sleight Problem

Stalwart hurtled to his feet, knocked over the chair, banged his head on a dangling net full of onions, and hit the back wall at a gallop. He would have hit it with both shoulders had it been possible for his head to fit in the air shaft. "Em? That you?"

"Sh! Can you hear me—I mean, are you free to move around?"

"Yes!" His heart pounded. Funny—he felt almost more scared now than he had before. Now he had a friend out there. Now, just maybe, there was a chance of *not* dying?

She whispered, "I heard what they were saying, Wart, most of it. I sent old Mervyn for help, but they won't get here until after dawn. Can you hang on until then somehow?"

Oh, *good* idea! As soon as help appeared in the valley, he would be tossed in the river. Dangerous evidence would never be left lying around Smealey Hole. He forced himself to speak slowly and calmly.

"Personally, I'm in no hurry, but they'll move as soon as the novices have gone to sleep." Owen had said that, implying that not all the residents of Smealey Hole were traitors. Stalwart would not repeat that to Emerald in case she developed some crazy idea of organizing a revolution. It would never work, because Eilir was certainly loyal to the Prior and his swordsmen controlled the valley. "Em, you've got to leave! One of us must survive to be a witness. Please go!" He found that horribly hard to say: *Please go away and leave me alone again.*

He was more frightened now than he had been in Quagmarsh. There he had been so buoyed up by his hatred of Thrusk that he'd had no time to despair. Besides, Thrusk had been a clod; Owen was freakishly clever. No one outsmarted Owen Smealey.

The whisper came again. "There's a grille over this vent."

"I know."

"If I can get it off, I could give you your sword. Do you want it?"

Want it? "Yes please." *Yesyesyesyesyes . . .* If he had *Sleight* in his hand, he'd take on Badger and Eilir both. He could hold the door against the whole troop of men-at-arms for hours. It would change everything. They'd have to burn him out. Mervyn's men coming at dawn . . . He tried not to cackle.

"Just a minute," she whispered. "I'll try a rock."

"Wait! I'll go and make a noise."

Emerald said, "Right."

Stalwart hurried across to the door. He could still hear faint voices out there, probably three of them. Men-at-arms soldiered for money and did not necessarily believe in their leader's cause. He thumped the chair against the planks. "Traitors!" he yelled. "You're going to lose your heads for this, all of you. I'm an officer of the Crown. Let me out and I'll see you get royal pardons!" And so on—bang, yell, bang, yell . . . His efforts were ignored. Owen would have selected the guards with his usual care.

Eventually the prisoner decided that he had given Emerald enough time. If she had not opened the air shaft by now, she couldn't. He went back to it. "Em?"

"Ready," she said. "Stand clear."

A faint scraping sound . . . then *Sleight's* needle point came into view. He reached out and clasped the steel lovingly, pulled . . . *Clink!* . . . It stopped. His heart hit the floor. He felt Emerald ease the blade back, turn it, try again. . . . But he could visualize *Sleight's* wide quillons and the narrow shaft and he knew that nothing was going to work. He would have known sooner if he had allowed himself to think about it. In a moment the blade was withdrawn.

"Wart?" Emerald whispered. "It won't fit."

"No." He must try to think clearly. Ironhall taught that courage wasn't just not being afraid, it was being afraid and doing your duty anyway. The more fear you felt, the braver you were. No shame in not wanting to die. Great honor in dying if you had to. "Nice try. Thanks. How much did you hear of what Badger said?"

"All of it, I think."

"Good. Then I needn't explain. I'm very grateful you came, but you really *must* go now! Please? Promise? No more heroics. It's very important that you get back safely to explain what happened. That sorcery is terrible! So please go now."

He probably wouldn't rank a mention in the *Litany of Heroes*, but it would be nice if *Sleight* got to hang in the sky of swords.

21 Faces from the Past

After leaving the prisoner, Badger and Eilir walked back to the residence in silence, not sharing their thoughts. Badger felt awkward without the weight of a sword at his side. He hated the stupid sorcerer's gown that Owen insisted he wear so he would not stand out and provoke questions. That was either an admission that not everyone in the Hole was completely trusted or just a reminder that Owen never completely trusted anyone.

As they walked into the candlelight entrance, the first person they saw was Owen himself—waiting for them, of course. Suspicious, of course. Standing so his hood shadowed his face, of course.

"Well?" he demanded.

"Nothing," Badger said.

The only reason Owen had let him go to speak with Wart was to find out if Wart had anything up his sleeve. Frighten a man enough and he might blurt out secrets. It was unheard of for Ironhall candidates to be taken from the school before their binding, so of course Owen suspected that Wart had not been totally honest. Owen could not imagine anyone being totally honest. He was convinced that the kid was just bait on a hook and the Old Blades were skulking around, waiting to pounce.

"I still want to know why Snake sent a boy!"

Badger groaned. "Just what I said before—the Old Blades are run off their feet and this Smealey lead was a long shot. They sent the boy because he wouldn't attract attention. Wart isn't capable of lying on that scale. Snake is, certainly, but the kid is scared spitless. If he knew anything about a rescue coming he'd have told us."

Owen's restless gaze flickered to Eilir.

"I agree," the one-eyed man said. "He didn't try to bribe me, which I expected, but I'm sure he just didn't think of it. He certainly wasn't gloating as if we'd fallen into a trap."

"He may not know about the trap."

"Prior," Eilir said patiently, "I really don't think there is a trap."

The sorcerer pouted. "Very well. Another half hour or so. Stay in here until then," he told Badger. He stalked away.

Without looking at Eilir, Badger headed for the stairs. Treads creaked as he climbed—the same treads that had creaked when he was a child: the third, eighth, twelfth. . . . Half an hour gave him just enough time to do what he wanted to do. His bones ached from lack of sleep, but that was not the main reason he felt so miserable.

He would not describe Wart as a close friend, or even a friend at all. He didn't have friends. But the kid was amusing company and not half-witted like some Ironhall inmates. He was a fine lutenist, juggler, acrobat. He'd earned his living as a minstrel's helper before he was even in his teens, whereas most of the others arrived there as useless trash. At times he had been a pest, but he didn't deserve this death. At least it would be quick, now that Owen had been talked out of his more savage intentions.

Carrying his lantern high ahead of him, Badger started up a second staircase, a very narrow one.

Kill Ambrose by all means. But to do it by killing another man—or boy—seemed so unfair! Not that Badger was about to insist on sparing Wart so he could carry out his own suicidal assassination plot. One way or another, Wart must die. He knew too much now. It was not a happy thought. All right for Owen; as a soldier, he'd killed before.

The stair brought him to a narrow, cramped space under the ridge of the roof. Low doors led to attics where servants had slept in the old days, but there were no servants in the Hole anymore, and the novices occupied the old field-workers' bunkhouses. Beyond these squalid sleeping quarters, angular nooks under the eaves provided hideaways for a billion spiders, storage for generations of junk, and play areas for small boys on wet days.

Badger went to the one he wanted and broke a fingernail prying open the access panel. It had not been moved since the day the last of the Smealeys were driven from their home. With less than an hour's warning that the Sheriff was on his way, they had hidden their most precious keepsakes in these attic cubbyholes—nothing of real value, though. Golden plates and silver candlesticks had stayed on display because the King's men would certainly have resorted to torture if they had not found the loot they expected. Here were only sentimental treasures, like the pictures Badger had come for. They were stacked exactly as he remembered leaving them. No one was less sentimental than Owen.

But the other things he had left on top of

them were still there too, because he had never told Owen or even Anwen about those. Sword, horn, and dagger—personal treasures Ceri had left in the hollow tree. The horn and sword were ordinary, but the dagger was special.

Ceri's claim to be rightful Prince of Nythia had relied on a very flimsy tale, the drunken ravings of a half-mad grandfather, and not the terrible Grandfather Gwyn, either. It was through Anwen that the royal pretension had come, descent from an illegitimate royal daughter, who had been ignored by historians and perhaps invented long after her death. No one had put much stock in this dubious ancestor, but she had been necessary, and had been accepted by the patriots. One of those supporters had presented Ceri with an ancient dagger bearing the green dragon emblem of the royal house of Nythia worked into the hilt in gold and jade. Ceri had worn it ever after, until that final night when he had shed his last hopes and finery and ridden off to ransom his mother and brothers. It was a beautiful thing still, and much too valuable to be abandoned. Owen should have it, for he was the pretender now, Prince of Nythia. Badger put it aside to take with him.

He took up the topmost portrait and held it near the glimmering lantern. The mice had pretty much ignored it; it had not warped or split. Because Edryd had preferred to work on sawn wooden panels, the portraits were all small, no more than heads and necks, not quite life-size. The first was of the artist himself, eyes fixedly staring out of the mirror he had used. And young! Of course Edryd could not have been much older then than Badger was now. That was an unwelcome surprise. He propped the panel against the wall and reached for the next, unable to remember the order in which he had left them, twelve long years ago.

The second picture was of Bevan himself, a grinning imp of a child with his silver lock prominent. No need to linger over that one.

The third was Aneirin. Poor, tortured Aneirin! Even then, in the golden days of youth before the uprising, life had never been easy for Aneirin. There had been voices and inexplicable changes of mood. Edryd had caught some of that agony in the lowered glance, the hint of sunken cheek.

Then Lloyd, the scholar, with chin cupped in ink-stained fingers, staring down at something not shown—a book, perhaps. Lloyd himself had long since returned to the elements, and only this likeness remained to show that he had ever existed.

Ceri was fifth. Again—how *young*! How very, astonishingly, young! Ceri looked no older than an Ironhall senior, but perhaps he had been only nineteen or twenty when he posed for his brother. Yet how magnificent, even then! The dark curls lapping the forehead, the line of jaw, eyes raised to horizons unseen by lesser mortals. The silver lock had been most marked on him—Ceri had excelled at everything, always. Even Edryd had been inspired to create a masterpiece when he painted that wonderful head, those shiny eyes, those lips about to speak.

How young! And how . . . How *what*? For a long time Badger held the panel, staring at it, teasing out every detail, analyzing it with the experience gained in the past twelve years—adolescence, the longest and most vital years in any man's life. . . . How *what*? What exactly was it he was seeing there that he had not expected? A dreamer? Yes, but he had always known Ceri was a dreamer. Leadership, of course. Intelligence. Courage. What else? Ruthlessness? Rather call it ambition. He had known his rebellion would cost many men's lives. He had known that his own chances must be least of all, and he had been willing to take that chance.

No, that still wasn't it. *Idealism?* Badger had never thought of Ceri as an idealist. He himself certainly wasn't. Childhood poverty as a foreigner in Isilond had wiped the stars from his eyes. Years of grind in Ironhall under self-imposed sentence of death had toughened him even further. Ceri had been a nobleman's son, raised in luxury. Maybe Ceri had really expected to find justice and liberty and kindness in this world. Amazing!

Time was up. They would be starting soon.

Badger left the hatch open and everything else where it lay. Only the dagger he tucked out of sight under his robe. Taking up the lantern, he headed back to the stair.

22

Point of View

Leaving poor Wart in his cell was the hardest thing Emerald had ever done. Since Quagmarsh she could never doubt his courage, yet he had not quite managed to suppress the quaver of dread in his voice. His arguments made sense—she could do no good there, and it was her duty now to see that the traitors were brought to justice. Sick at heart, she wriggled off through the weeds until she was far enough from the watchers' fire to risk standing up; then she picked her way through the dark behind the hay shed, waving the rapier in front of her as she had before.

She had promised Wart very faithfully that she would make her own escape now and wait for the promised rescue that would come too late to save him. Or save the King! As she made her stumbling way around the complex of buildings, she realized that Wart had been wrong. Justice must wait. Her first duty was to save the King, who was also destined to die before dawn. And it was then that she sensed again the magic aura of the octogram.

The big building had changed. Earlier it had been dark and deserted. Now a faint flicker of firelight showed through the open door. The elementary was being made ready for the conjuration. She went closer, trying to ignore that cloying stench of sorcery. Standing on tiptoe, she peered through a window slit. The thickness of the wall restricted her view to a fire burning in an open hearth near the center and colored banners hung on the wall opposite. Nothing more.

She hurried around the back, stubbing her toes and shins several times in the process. There the ground was a little higher, and the window holes were dark, so there must be a separate room back there. She found one slit a little wider than the others, where the logs had rotted. It was a very tight squeeze, and the sword hindered her, but she managed to scramble through.

The rear chamber was an afterthought, cut off from the main hall by a jerry-built partition of rotting planks. At the cost of a few more bruises, she established that it was furnished with benches; she concluded that the

Fellowship used it as a classroom. That might not be its only purpose, though. If it also served as storage or a dressing room, then the adepts were liable to walk in on her at any minute. She put an eye to a chink in the wall and inspected the main room again.

The fire wafted white smoke upward. Now she could see the octogram outlined on the flagstones, but the building was clearly a heroes' mead hall left over from days of yore. A sort of cloister along one side puzzled her until she realized that it was another addition, a gallery for spectators or musicians. It sagged in places and some of the posts supporting it were canted at odd angles, so obviously it was no longer in use. The stair to it began right outside the door beside her. If she could hide up there, she decided, she would be safer and see better. She would be almost directly above the conjuration. Even if she could not find a way to stop the evil, it would be a good place to hide until the Sheriff's men arrived.

Too late! Voices came drifting in the main doorway, followed by the speakers themselves, two male novices in white robes. One of them carried a sledgehammer, and had probably been chosen for the breadth of his shoulders. They were grumbling in the manner of prideful young men set to do servants' work. When they reached the center of the octogram, the smaller man crouched and positioned something he had brought with him. He steadied it while his companion tapped it down with the hammer. Once it was secure, the little man stepped back and Shoulders swung his hammer in earnest. The hall shuddered. Dust cascaded down from the roof; a cloud of bats whirled in squeaks of protest and drained out the windows. The two men walked away, still grousing. Where they had been working stood a shiny metal staple.

Emerald was again alone. Moving as fast as those frightened bats had, she slipped out of the smaller room and scrambled up the stairs to the gallery. As she reached the top, a lurch and loud creaks warned her that she had made a foolhardy move. Under an ancient layer of bat guano, the planks were worm-eaten and rotted. One gave way, her right foot went through, and she sprawled headlong on the filth. The platform swayed, then steadied.

Bearing lighted lanterns, a line of sorcerers and swordsmen came trooping into the elementary. She was trapped on a most precarious perch.

23 Change of Heart

The night had turned frosty, but there was no wind. The waning moon floated like a boat above the cliffs. Hurrying across to the elementary, Badger could see the window slits drooling ribbons of white smoke upward, and another cloud rising from the watch fire outside Wart's prison. Despite the fire, the interior of the elementary was still quite dark; the lanterns hung around the walls glowed like stars in the miasma of woodsmoke. He saw seventeen swordsmen—Ironhall training made him count them—and three novices in white robes plus a dozen adepts, barely visible in their black. One of those was Owen, scrutinizing every face that came in the doorway and issuing orders to Eilir at the same time.

" . . . and leave no more than six in here," he concluded.

"I thought you had the whole complex

warded?" the Sergeant grumbled.

"There are ways they can bypass the warding if they bring sorcerers with them."

"Do you ever worry about wolves in the woods 'round here?"

"There have been no wolves in Chivial for a hundred years," Owen snapped. "Nor in Nythia either."

"No one's *seen* any, you mean. Who's to say they haven't just learned how to look like squirrels?"

"Do as you're told!"

"Yes, Your Malevolence." Eilir raised his voice in a bellow. "Gruffydd, boy! Stay you here with all your troop. The rest of you fine lads come with me. Going to freeze the buttons off your britches, we are." He strode out and the men-at-arms reluctantly followed him, all but five. It was a chilly night for picket duty.

Owen scowled at his brother.

Badger scowled back. "How long will this take?"

"An hour or more, once we get started. It's a very complex conjuration. Maybe longer."

It would be almost dawn.

"Well, you don't need me. I'll go and feed the bedbugs for a while." Badger was out on his feet. He had not slept for two nights, and had not slept *well* for two weeks before that. Owen expected him to set out for Buran at first light and keep going until he arrived at Grandon—and then he would need all his wits about him whether the King was alive or dead. Yet he saw the instant veil of distrust fall over his brother's face.

"Why? Is your conscience troubling you?"

"Of course not."

"You should be here to witness our triumph. I want you here."

"As you wish." Badger sighed and added under his breath, "I see why Eilir called you Malevolence." He strode off across the hall with his absurd gown swishing around his ankles.

The adepts stood around under lanterns, alone or in small groups, reviewing sheafs of paper, which he assumed spelled out their spells for them. He had not seen the hall in use since the great day of Ceri's proclamation. For no better reason than that he wandered all the way to the corner by the gallery stair and placed himself directly below the spot where he had hidden that night to watch the birth of the revolution. The crowd then had been bigger, noisier, infinitely drunker—several hundred armed men on benches swilling mead and ale, singing patriotic songs, cheering every word of the speeches. Especially Ceri's speech. *Liberty!* he had declaimed. *Justice! Down with foreign overlords, and foreign taxes. Ancient rights. Ancestral freedoms* . . . The applause had echoed from the hills and shaken the old ruin to its foundations.

Crazy youthful idealism! With childish trust, young Bevan had believed every word of it. The older, cynical Badger did not and was quite shocked to realize that Ceri might have believed it himself.

Ironhall lectures about Nythia had been straight Chivian propaganda, but some of the ancient knights who moldered in unneeded corners had been knowledgeable and willing to speak out in private conversations. Although he had needed to be cautious in what he admitted knowing, he had enjoyed a talk or two with old Sir Clovis. The snarly old veteran had insisted that Ceri's worst mistake had been his tolerance of those who refused to support him. "Should have chopped off some heads," the old tiger had claimed. "Wiped out the fence-sitters. Gotten everyone behind him."

Ceri would never have done that.

And Ceri would never have done what Owen was doing tonight.

Badger's reverie was interrupted by the arrival of four men-at-arms and the prisoner.

Wart was invisible inside a black gown comically too large for him, trailing on the ground. He tripped frequently, but two of the bull-size guards had hold of his arms, almost carrying him. Another led him by a tether, like an animal.

Owen followed them to the octogram, where they pushed the captive down on his knees and tied his leash to the staple. The Prior inspected the knots and then sent the guards out to join Eilir and his pickets. He glanced around the elementary to see who remained.

"Adepts take your places. The rest of you will remain absolutely silent. And do not wander around. This is a long enchantment. If you want to sit, do so now."

Four men and four women took up position within the octogram, one at each point, all clutching their scripts. Four more adepts, three novices, and five swordsmen remained standing around the walls in ones or twos. No one sat down.

A small fragment of wood bounced off Badger's shoulder and dropped at his feet. Surprised, he looked down and saw others, plus a few larger splinters, a small heap of guano. The old gallery must be about ready to collapse, which would not be unexpected. There might be mice at work. . . .

Was that a very faint *creak*?

How big a mouse did it take to make a floor creak?

There was someone up there.

"Ready?" Owen proclaimed, and cleared his throat. "In your incantations you should find that the words 'the donor, Lord Digby' have been corrected in all cases to 'the donor, King Ambrose.' We think we have caught every instance, but please watch in case we—"

"Wait!" Badger shouted.

He strode over toward Wart without thinking. Or thinking, rather, of so many things at one time that he didn't know which was which. He needed time to work it all out. Owen had been right—there was an ambush, whether Wart knew of it or not. There had to be. *Snake already had men hidden up there in the gallery!* They had bypassed the wards; they were in the compound. Eilir and his men outside were probably under arrest already or just plain dead, if the Old Blades were capable of cutting throats by night. As soon as the adepts began their conjuration, the tigers would pounce on them also.

The cause was already lost. That was an astonishing relief.

"What do think you're doing?" Owen roared.

"You swore there would be no torture!" Badger roared back. "You've left his hands tied. I've seen Ambrose's wrists and they're fat as hams. And the boy still has boots on—they'll crush his feet."

He reached the prisoner and bent to look at him. Wart was obviously uncomfortable, doubled over on his knees with his hands behind his back, folded like a trussed chicken. The jeweled star was pinned on his shoulder.

"Flames!" Owen shouted. "Take off his cursed boots if you want. Leave him tied there, though! And hurry up!"

Badger checked the noose to make sure it was wide enough not to strangle Wart when the sorcery made his neck larger. He drew Ceri's dagger and bent to cut the bonds around the slender, boyish wrists. Remembering Ambrose's, he winced when he saw how the binding had already dug into the flesh.

"Thanks," Wart mumbled. He put his hands on the floor to ease the strain on his back.

Badger went down on one knee to remove Wart's boots. "I'll leave you the knife," he whispered. "Make a break for it when you get the chance." He pulled off the boots and threw them out of the octogram. Then he rose and stalked back to his former place. In the darkness no one had seen him slide the dagger in under the folds of the prisoner's gown.

"If we may now proceed?" Owen said sarcastically. "The words, 'the gifted horn' should have been changed throughout the incantations to 'the gifted star.' Otherwise there are no changes. First canto begins with fire and air in unison. Ready? One, two—"

Badger felt better. Ceri would have applauded what he had just done. Ceri would have detested this perverted, sorcerous vengeance. True, by giving Wart at least a sporting chance in the coming fight, Badger was following the family tradition of treachery, betraying his brother and his oath, but he took comfort in knowing that the cause was hopeless now. He waited tensely for the Blades hiding in the gallery to make their move.

24 Stalwart Stalwart

Emerald had known some bad moments in her life, especially in the last two weeks, but this had to be the worst ever. She lay facedown in filth whose dust stung her eyes and tickled her nose, so she perpetually needed to sneeze. As a witness to treason, she was in fearful danger. She was already developing cramps, but any attempt to find a more comfortable position wrung squeaks and protests out of the dilapidated structure. Mere breathing seemed almost enough to shake it and send showers of dirt dribbling down through the rotten planks. Now she faced the horrors of the conjuration itself. After spending four years becoming attuned to the subtlest variations in the elements, she would find interrogation on the rack mere child's play compared to witnessing a major enchantment at close quarters.

As the adepts began their invocations, she

gingerly raised her head to look. She could not see Badger, but she knew he was standing right below her, because she had almost died of fright when he called out. There were half a dozen men-at-arms scattered around the hall, plus a dozen or so male and female sorcerers. Wart was helpless, a huddled heap in the center of the octogram. That left only her to fight for the right. Bad odds!

Wart was facing toward her, his face invisible under the hood of his robe. She could think of no way to free him and pass him his sword, and even if she could, the odds were impossible, even for him. Light flashed. . . . What?

Then again.

Apparently no one but Emerald noticed anything—everyone else was intent on the enchantment, and she was looking down, at a very different angle. *Again!* Wart, she realized, was surreptitiously cutting through his tether and the light she was seeing was torchlight reflected from the blade of his knife. How had he gotten hold of a knife? That could have happened only in the few minutes between the time Emerald left him in his cell and the guards' coming to fetch him. His rapier had been too wide for the air hole, but a knife or dagger could have been passed in easily enough.

Who? It could only be Mervyn and his men, no one else. They had arrived already! Perhaps not all of them, just an advance scout or two. She could not imagine how they had passed by the warding spells unnoticed, but if anyone could do it, who else but foresters? So the rest of them would be on their way. Rescue was coming!

By the time she had worked that out, the elementals had begun to answer the enchanters' call and the resulting spirituality drove every other thought from her head. Owen and his accomplices were ripping apart the fabric of the world. The discordance assaulted her senses, blinding, deafening, choking. It skewed all eight elements, violating every principle of balance and harmony, but its main components were love and fire, as the Sisters in the court had reported. Love was elemental in all relationships between people, and forcing one man into an exact replica of another was to forge the closest relationship imaginable. Fire included light and hence vision, and so was required to change his appearance. Air elementals could make him sound like the King, water would reflect his likeness . . . and so on. As an example of the art of conjury it was a masterpiece, but it was also utter evil.

She felt as if she were being spun around, beaten with iron rods, choked, burned, and frozen, all at the same time. She needed to scream for them to stop, yet she must not move a finger. She had never heard of a conjuration so long and complicated. A single performance would have taken a couple of hours. But, like all spells, it had to be recited perfectly, and three times one of the chanters made a mistake. Each time the Prior cursed and ordered them to begin again at the beginning.

Where were the foresters? Why didn't they hurry?

By the time Emerald's ordeal ended, a dim light beyond the windows told of the first tremors of dawn. Even the sorcerers seemed to welcome the release, for they lapsed into total silence. In that blissful stillness, she heard birds tuning up their morning chorus.

Fighting giddiness and nausea, she dared to raise her head and look. Wart had gone. A much larger man had taken his place, for the black gown that had flopped so loose around him now strained across a massively rounded back. A thin cheer from the sorcerers confirmed that the conjuration had succeeded.

"Magnificent, brothers and sisters!" the Prior shouted, hoarse from long chanting. "Gruffydd, go and bring Eilir and the others so that they may witness this historic justice. Gather 'round, all of you, and watch the tyrant's execution." Carrying a huge two-handed broadsword, he marched forward to the helpless prisoner. The others drew close also. Man-at-arms Gruffydd headed for the door.

Why were Mervyn's foresters not doing something? Very gently, trying not to make the gallery shake, Emerald drew Wart's sword from its scabbard. If somebody did not do something to save him soon, she would have to watch him die. Do what, though? All she could think of was to throw him the rapier. Thoughts of hurling it like a javelin and impaling the odious Owen were pure wishful thinking. Having never fenced in her life, she could not hope to rush down and slaughter five men-at-arms. Most of the adepts wore swords, as well. Mervyn and his men were going to be too late, for Wart's life would end as soon as the Prior tired of gloating. He set the monstrous sword vertically on its point right in front of the prisoner's eyes. Resting his arms on the wide quillons, he gazed down, feasting his eyes on his victim.

In spite of his wretchedly cramped position,

Stalwart had not been idle during the conjuration. Badger's gift of the dagger had put new life into him, or at least some hope of extending his present life. It was wonderful to realize that he had *not* been wrong to trust his friend! Whatever reasons had led Badger to return to Smealey Hole instead of going back to Buran, he was one of the good guys after all. His whispered remark about making a break for it meant that there was going to be a rescue attempt. After some thought, Stalwart had remembered the hints that not all the inhabitants of the Hole were traitors. So Badger had somehow organized a revolt. When the time was ripe, he would give the signal for the loyalists to rise and overthrow mad Owen.

The time did not ripen quickly. While the sorcerers wailed their enchantment, Stalwart surreptitiously sawed through his tether, leaving a few threads intact so it would look right. After a while he began to feel giddy—heart pounding, arms and legs twitching. He thought he was just having cramps until a tightening of his robe warned him that the magic was changing him. He was growing! For years he had been wanting to grow—but not like this. He could feel his belly expanding like a wineskin being filled.

When the chanting stopped, the first light of

morning was creeping into the elementary. His head had cleared, but now his cramps were real. He was not at all sure he could stand up without help, or at least a few minutes to stretch his muscles, and the traitors would never allow that. Soon they would notice the almost-severed rope. Why were Badger and his friends not doing something?

He heard Owen summon Eilir and his men. Then a broadsword touched the flagstones in front of him.

"Well, Sir Stalwart?" said the Prior's odious voice. "How does it feel to be a king, mm? I fear we cannot allow you long to enjoy your new status, because we must flush your remains down the Hole before sunup. You did swear to die for your King, didn't you? Aren't you happy to have the chance?"

Chuckling, steadying the sword with one hand, he bent to peer in his victim's face.

With a roar that astonished even him—and was partly a scream of pain—Stalwart sprang up, snapping the last threads of his tether. He grabbed the hilt of the broadsword and simultaneously slashed the dagger at the sorcerer. He would have killed him had his limbs not cramped up on him so much, or had Owen not turned out to be so much *smaller* than he expected. Nevertheless, the Prior squealed and fell back with blood spurting from a gashed arm. Onlookers howled in horror.

"Execution?" King Ambrose's voice thundered through the hall. "If there's to be executions, I'll do the executing." Two-handed, Stalwart swung the broadsword at the conjurer, but again his stiff limbs betrayed him. He stumbled and missed. Owen was already backing away, fumbling to draw the sword that hung at his side.

Boots hammered on the stairs at Emerald's back. The gallery groaned, rocking like a cockleshell in a tidal bore.

Seeing another scythe stroke coming, the Prior dodged, dropped his sword, and fled. The King lumbered after him, swinging the broadsword around as if it weighed no more than a riding crop.

Man-at-arms Gruffydd bellowed, "Kill him!" and charged. His followers and the armed adepts drew their swords also, but with less enthusiasm.

Emerald turned and saw Badger's horrified face staring at her. The platform began to shift one way and the stair another.

Gruffydd closed with Stalwart and stopped a killer swipe that brushed aside his attempt to parry and practically cut him in half. "One!" roared the King.

Badger howled, "The sword!"

Emerald hurled the rapier to him an instant before the gallery collapsed. She slid, yelled, clutched at the teetering railing, and then shot down in an avalanche of rotten timber and filth. An explosion of dust shot out, filling the entire elementary with foul and acrid fog.

That saved the day.

For a few minutes everybody was blinded. Badger began yelling a war cry of, "Starkmoor! Starkmoor!" between coughs, and the King took it up. Everyone else was enemy, so the two of them laid about them at will, hunting down and striking every blurred shape. A few voices countered with, "Nythia! Nythia!" but those were rapidly silenced or turned into screams.

Emerald felt safest just lying where she had fallen. Only when she was sure she had not broken any bones did she stand up, choking and weeping. By that time, the battle was over. The last fugitive sorcerers had vanished, taking their wounded. Badger and the King stood in the doorway, howling derision after them.

Three adepts, one novice, and five men-at-arms lay dead on the floor. She noticed that none of the adepts wore the Prior's gold belt.

The victims of Wart's butchering broadsword were easily distinguished by their gaping wounds and the pools of blood around them. It seemed only three of the nine had been felled by Badger's surgically precise rapier. The two victors lowered their blades, looked at each other, and then whooped louder than ever. They crashed together in an embrace and a dance of triumph. The King lifted Badger off his feet and swung him around.

Ignoring her bruises, Emerald hobbled over to the capering lunatics at the door. "Wart?"

"Em! Are you all right?"

"Are you Wart?"

"Of course I'm Stalwart." He thumped his prominent belly. "*Exceedingly* stalwart!"

He might think he was Wart. To look at he was King Ambrose—huge and fat and loud, but capable of twirling Badger around like a child without even laying down that broadsword. He filled the sorcerer's gown beyond capacity, for it had split at the shoulders and barely met across his bulging belly, exposing a tangle of reddish fur on his chest. Although he seemed to be unwounded, he was splattered with other men's blood from his bare feet to his bronze beard. His globular face was coated with the foul gray dust, showing red streaks where sweat had run down it. He was gasping and panting, but his piggy little eyes gleamed with triumph. He reeked of the evil sorcery.

"Whoever he is," Badger said, "he wields a broadsword like a rapier. Very nice counter-disengagement on that last exchange, Your Grace."

The King beamed down at him. "Thank you, my boy. You're a deft hand with a rapier when you have to be. We hereby appoint you commander of our personal—"

"Idiots!" she shouted. "There's another dozen swordsmen around somewhere!"

"Well? The lady has a point. Will they fight or run?"

Badger sighed. "Now they have friends to avenge. Owen won't give up."

"I'd hate to think we just won a battle only to lose the war." The voice was the King's, but the note of worry in it was Wart's. "It's not light yet, so we—"

"Look out!" Emerald yelled.

Sergeant Eilir and another man charged out of the twilight. They had donned proper battle gear—breastplates and steel helmets—and they carried shields. With that advantage, those seasoned veterans must have expected to dispose of untried, unarmored boys before they could work up a decent sweat. But their opponents were fresh from four years' training in the world's finest swordsmanship. They jumped forward to confine the attackers in the narrow doorway.

Eilir had put himself on the left so his blind side would be partly covered by his companion's shield. He was a large and powerful man, but he did not compare to King Ambrose. He tried to block Wart's broadsword stroke with his buckler, but the sheer power of the blow sliced it open from the top edge down almost to his arm and made him stagger. The other man parried Badger's rapier successfully, but before he could riposte it flashed back again, stabbing at his groin. While he blocked that stroke, his shield caught on Eilir's shoulder. Badger's next lunge poked deep into his eye. The falling body fouled the Sergeant, who stumbled and was chopped down by Wart.

"Eleven!" roared Wart. "Who's next?"

Emerald grabbed him with both hands and pulled him back into the shadows—the hall was now darker than the yard outside.

"That should slow them down a little," he said, puffing hard.

"Some, but not Owen," Badger said. "Come on!" He ran toward the far end of the hall.

* * *

Stalwart lumbered after him, feeling like a moving haystack. Size and strength were an enjoyable novelty, but he had lost his speed and that was not a good exchange. He was in very real danger still, which meant that the King was.

The elementary was too enormous to be defended by only two. Men with axes could easily chop away the rotten logs to enlarge the window slits and make a dozen extra doors. If the traitors just tossed a flaming torch in on the ruins of the gallery and turned the place into a furnace, it would burn like tinder. Would anyone in Waterby have listened to old Mervyn's story? His rescue was not due until dawn, if it came at all. Dawn at the cliff top. It would take him and his companions time to reach the Hall, and Owen might have set guards on the path.

Stalwart followed Emerald into the back room. Badger was already hauling on a brass ring set in the floor, lifting one of the slabs to reveal empty darkness below.

25

Secret Passage

The hatch thudded shut overhead and cut off all traces of light. Standing at the bottom of the steps, Emerald could not even see Wart right beside her.

"I don't like this!" growled the King's voice. "We're trapped!"

"There's a bolt here," Badger's voice said from the top, "so they can't follow us." His boots tapped softly as he felt his way down. "This is an escape hole; it locks on this side."

"Where does it go?"

"Just out to the riverbank, not far. Give your eyes a moment and you'll see some light, I think."

The air was dank, as if somehow dusty and moldy at the same time. Somewhere water dripped steadily. Emerald enjoyed the solid, safe feeling of a cave. So would Badger, but it would be torture to an air person like Wart.

"This is the secret passage you told us about? And who else knows of it?"

"Only us and one other in the world, I expect," Badger said sadly. "I think this is why the old elementary was never pulled down—the owners, whoever they were, always liked to keep their back door a secret."

"Owen knows of it, you mean. So he'll cut us off."

"He may have forgotten."

"Nonsense!" Wart snarled, and Emerald agreed with him. Owen Smealey would never forget a secret back door.

"Hold on to me," Badger said, "and watch you don't bang your crowned head, Your Grace."

Emerald laid a hand on Wart's shoulder to complete the chain. She thought the cave must be natural originally, but its floor had been smoothed, perhaps paved. The walls felt rough to her touch as she felt her way with her free hand.

"It'll be too light outside to make a run for the hills," Badger murmured, his voice echoing eerily. "We'll have to wait for Mervyn."

"If he ever shows up."

* * *

When they rounded a bend and saw a gray shimmer of light on the floor, Stalwart felt a huge rush of relief. He hated this rabbiting around underground.

"Let's sit down and wait," Badger suggested. "We can hold this place against an army."

"No!" Stalwart said. "If I were your sweet brother I'd smoke us out like wasps or bury us alive. I'm going out to have a look." The exit was a narrow shaft sloping steeply upward. He was not even sure he could get his bloated body through that crevice. Ignoring the others' protests, he laid down his broadsword and made the attempt.

It was a very tight squeeze. He had to put his arms ahead of him and wriggle on his belly, but in a moment he scrambled out into a natural alcove in the rocky riverbank. Black and deadly, the swift- flowing Smealey ran twenty feet or so below him. The sky was blue, close to sunrise. To his left he could see upriver, across a wide meadow to distant hills. He assumed the foresters would be coming from the opposite direction if they came at all. His view that way was blocked by a spur of the cliff, but there was a sort of path around it, a very narrow ledge. Normally he could cheerfully have run along that while juggling flaming torches, but at the moment he was a very fat man, made unsteady by an unfamiliar body.

So he went slowly and carefully, watching where he placed his bare feet. He had hardly started when Owen screamed in triumph and jumped him.

He had been waiting just around the corner. As Stalwart staggered under the impact, the madman crushed him in his massive, horseshoe-bending arms. He laughed, hatred burning in his eyes.

"Die, King Ambrose! They'll find you drowned in your bed. Take me with you if you can—I won't care." Owen made to hurl King Ambrose off the ledge.

"I care!" Stalwart bellowed. He twisted and slammed them both against the rocky wall. He was on the outside, of course.

Owen uttered a choking gasp of dismay. He pushed them both away from the jagged surface. Stalwart smashed him back into it again. Panic flickered in the sorcerer's eyes—obviously he had no experience at wrestling bulls. He should have stamped on Stalwart's vulnerable bare feet, but he didn't. When his head and kidneys were ground against the rocks a third time, his grip weakened. Ambrose pounded him bodily against the cliff a fourth time for luck, then prized him loose. He held Owen out over the river and let go. The sorcerer vanished in silence, with barely a splash. Smealey River swallowed another Smealey and flowed on as if nothing had happened.

Alone again, Stalwart leaned back against the rock to catch his breath and wipe the sweat off his face. Even though he was due for a little good luck for a change, that had been an unpleasantly close call. Owen had been in too much of a hurry to reach the exit and block the fugitives' escape, he assumed, and had not waited to round up help, or even a replacement sword.

Meanwhile he hoped the King was not about to have a heart attack. There were certainly advantages in having some weight to throw around. Owen ought to be going over the falls just about now. . . .

But he had won! With Eilir and Owen and so many others dead, the traitors would surely flee now. He must keep himself safe for the King's sake, but surely he could send Badger to rally the loyalists and take over the Hall.

"What are you doing?" Emerald emerged from the cave.

"Just admiring a sunrise I had not expected to—what's that?" He turned to peer upstream.

It was not a hunting horn, it was a bugle. Dawn sun flashed off shiny breastplates and helmets; it blazed on flying banners and rainbow plumes. Hooves thundered. A troop of about fifty lancers came galloping across the meadow.

"Rescue!" Emerald yelled. "The King's men!"

"Oh, *pus*!" Wart said. "Pus and *puke*! Yeomen! Household Yeomen!"

Why did *this* have to happen, just when things were going so well?

Ten minutes later, the cavalry was milling around in the yard. The leader, who swung nimbly down from his foaming charger, was not clad in the armor of the Household Yeomen. Nor was he wearing his customary scarlet robes and golden chain, but there was no mistaking his air of authority. He looked around the complex, then strode over to the corpses lying in the door of the elementary. He stopped and stared incredulously as Emerald emerged, stepping over Eilir's body.

"Sister!" Durendal bowed.

Remembering that the filthy rags she was wearing were the remains of a man's costume, not a woman's, she bowed in return. "Welcome to Smealey Hole, Lord Chancellor!"

"Have I arrived too late for the excitement?"

"A few hours earlier would have been preferable." She forced a smile, but she knew that she was on the brink of collapse. "You are a most welcome sight all the same, my lord."

Why and how he came to be leading this troop of lancers did not matter. He was in control now, and all would be well.

Badger stepped out of the shadowed doorway and raised *Sleight* in salute.

It was an article of faith around court in Chivial that no face was more inscrutable then the Lord Chancellor's. Negotiators from a score of countries and factions could testify that the only emotions he ever displayed were those he chose to display. But his eyebrows did rise as he noted the bloodstains and that telltale silver curl. He would certainly recall the long-ago battle outside Waterby that had established his reputation as the greatest Blade of them all. He scowled at the cat's-eye on the hilt of the rapier. He frowned at the blood-smeared face.

"I've seen you before . . . not Guard . . ."

"In Ironhall, Lord Chancellor," Emerald said. "May I have the honor of presenting Prime Candidate Badger?"

Badger nodded ironically. "Formerly Bevan

Smealey of Smealey Hole. You met some of my brothers once."

Lord Roland definitely let slip a blink of surprise at that news. Then he looked up at the third figure emerging.

History was made. He paled. His eyes bulged. His jaw dropped.

"About time, Chancellor!" boomed King Ambrose. "What kept you, man? We have been seriously inconvenienced by your tardiness. No, don't bother to kneel."

26

The Fall of the House of Smealey

When the story had been told, two lancers the size of fir trees conducted Badger over to a bunkhouse. He fell on the first bed he saw and slept until nightfall, and even then it was only hunger that woke him. Washed, changed, and fed, he began to feel alive again. He hoped that this condition would not be too transient.

Still under guard, he was taken to the office in the residence to face Lord Roland, and on the way there he met a second procession, comprising King Ambrose and another four troopers, although in his case they would be more bodyguards than jailers. Bewilderingly, the King flashed Wart's smile at him. He was still dressed as an adept, in a cowled robe far too small for him. Perhaps there were no clothes in Nythia large enough to fit that king-sized bulk, or perhaps Lord Roland just wanted to keep the famous face concealed as much as possible.

Badger was comforted to know that there would be a witness present, because he was well aware that his troubles were far from over. A lot of difficult questions need never be asked if the last of the Smealeys just accidentally fell in the river.

Sister Emerald was already present, seated on a stool, chatting with the Chancellor across the table. Her baggage must have arrived from Waterby, for she was decked out in the snowy robes and tall hennin of the Sisterhood. She had seemed wrong as a boy, too diffident, although certainly stubborn enough. As a young woman she conveyed confidence and determination, without being in any way unfeminine. Not every bachelor at court was going to crash at her feet, Badger thought, but the toll would be heavy.

The weary, red-eyed Chancellor had certainly not lain abed all day like his visitors. The table's snowdrift of papers had been sorted into piles; the candles were well burned down already. He did not rise when the two men were ushered in; for a moment it seemed they would be left standing. Then two more stools arrived and the door was closed. Four occupants crowded the poky chamber like a beehive.

Roland looked them over. "I was just congratulating Sister Emerald on her courage and loyalty. She is absolutely the only person who comes out of this affair with credit." He shot a pointed glance at Sir Stalwart. "My lady, I have ordered a carriage to take you into Lomouth in the morning, where the Sisters can provide hospitality and further transportation."

"That is very kind of you, my lord." She was not blushing or preening. She had accepted the praise as her due, but she would not let success go to her head—unlike a certain Blade currently present.

"I left strict orders that the transfer of Peachyard to your mother be treated as a matter of urgency. The deeds will be ready by the time you reach Grandon. You do understand that this Smealey affair and your part in it must never become public knowledge?"

Durendal turned to Badger and the smiles ended. "I have more questions for you, Master Smealey."

Badger made himself hold that dark gaze without flinching. "I shall answer them if I can, Your Excellency."

"By accompanying Stalwart from Ironhall, you tacitly put yourself under his command. If you found the situation intolerable, you should have told him so and returned at once to Ironhall. Instead, you accepted his instructions to go and report to Sir Snake. Then you disobeyed. You came here, to Smealey Hole."

Badger nodded. He was determined not to beg for his life. If he had to die on the block like Ceri, he would do it proudly. Honor and duty and loyalty had failed him. Courage was all he had left.

Never changing his piercing stare, Roland continued, "You must have betrayed him to the sorcerers, since they knew the significance of the brooch. But then you gave him a knife so he could free himself. You fought at his side. Will you explain your purposes, when and why you changed your loyalties, and where they lie now?"

Badger shrugged. "Who can say exactly why he does anything? Motives may be very complex, Lord Chancellor."

The great Durendal did not like that answer. "You are a cynic. I have always found duty to be adequate motive."

"Duty? I was brought up to believe that my duty was to kill King Ambrose by any means whatsoever, even at the cost of my own life. My mother made me swear to it on her deathbed."

There was a silence.

"I see," Lord Roland said coldly. "And where lies your duty now?"

Badger had not thought about it. He took a moment to do so. "I cannot see that I have any duty or prospects in Chivial, my lord, so I suppose I must seek those elsewhere—if that option is available to me." That was as close as he would go to asking for mercy.

The Chancellor lifted a paper from a pile and passed it across. It was a declaration by Bevan Smealey, son of the late Baron Modred of Smealey, that he waived all claim to the lands and defunct baronetcy of Smealey, and also any claim that any member of his family had formerly advanced to royal status or the overlordship of Nythia; that he would now quit the realm of Chivial and Nythia with all possible dispatch; that he would never return, nor ever take up arms against the King of Chivial, Prince of Nythia; and that he signed under no duress or compulsion. That last bit was probably only true so long as he did not ask what the alternative was, but it was a shrewdly worded document.

He reached across for a quill, dipped it in the inkwell, and signed.

"Sister," said the Chancellor, "would you be so kind as to sign also, as witness? Thank you." He sifted sand on the ink. "And would you graciously allow Master Smealey to ride in your coach to Lomouth tomorrow? Now the Baelish treaty has been agreed, he should have no trouble finding a ship."

He tossed a purse. Badger caught it and knew by the weight that it held gold. The clouds were lifting faster than he had believed possible. He would live! He was going free! Just for a moment—and because he was a Smealey in Smealey Hole—he wondered if all this might be some sort of trap. But when he looked again at Durendal, even he could not believe that. The man's integrity almost glowed. No one could doubt that he deserved his reputation, or that nine tenths of the government of Chivial was present on the far side of the table.

"Your Excellency is most generous."

Astonishingly, Sister Emerald demurred. She was a very determined young lady. "Surely he may be given a little time to arrange his affairs, Lord Chancellor? Whatever his actions yesterday, Chivial owes him a considerable debt for what he did this morning."

"I have no affairs to settle, my lady," Badger said quickly. "I speak fluent Isilondian; I am an Ironhall-trained swordsman. I shall not starve." And tomorrow he would ask her to halt the coach for a moment beside the hollow tree.

He would go forth to seek his fortune with a good sword at his side.

"Then I shall be happy to see you to the docks."

Roland's manner had thawed a little. "Of course you will have a mounted escort tomorrow, Sister, and it will make sure that he does as he has promised. If I may presume to ask one last favor? When you see Master Smealey embark, would you then—and only then—give him this package?"

It was anonymous, wrapped in cloth, but just the right size to be a dagger with a green dragon worked into the hilt.

"You are more than generous, my lord," Badger said thickly. He had hoped for leniency. He had not expected generosity. He had never met it before. He did not know how to deal with it.

Roland's dark stare suggested that he had guessed as much. "As Sister Emerald says, we owe you a debt in the end. I warn you that I will burn this place to the ground before I leave. Not a stone will remain standing, and the land will be included in the royal forest of Brakwood. If there is anything else you wish to take from here, ask now."

He had found the paintings.

Badger hesitated, then said, "Nothing. Burn it all."

The door closed behind Badger and Emerald. Stalwart stayed where he was because he had been told to do so. The next few minutes were going to be tricky and his temporary resemblance to King Ambrose was not going to help him one little bit. Durendal was giving him the basilisk stare treatment. When in doubt, attack . . .

"May I inquire, my lord, how you managed to arrive so opportunely this morning?"

"No. Do you recognize my authority to give you orders?"

Technically a government minister had absolutely no authority over a Blade in the Royal Guard. This was no time to be technical.

"I will do whatever you say, my lord." There were three, and only three, Blades in the Order he must not address as "brother"—Leader, Grand Master, and the present Lord Chancellor, and he only because he was Durendal, not because of his office.

"Tomorrow," the great man said, "you and your escort will move to one of the royal hunting lodges, and there you will remain until you are yourself again—a matter of a week or so, according to the prisoners. During that time, you will be subject to the orders of Ensign Rolf. You will obey him in every respect, without argument or reservation. Is that clear, Sir Stalwart?"

Stalwart cringed. "A Yeoman?" If the Guard ever heard about this he would be ruined.

Roland's stare had grown even more menacing. "Have I your word on it?"

Sigh! "Yes, my lord."

"Three nights ago I congratulated you on the success of your first mission. I am considerably less impressed by your second."

Stalwart wiped his streaming forehead. His current body did sweat a lot. It was also perpetually hungry. He had eaten two enormous meals and was still starving.

"I may have let my earlier success make me a little overconfident."

"A *little*?"

In Stalwart's considered opinion, he had met with a lot of bad luck, but only a ninny blamed his luck. "I should have listened to Sister Emerald. And yet, in the end, I was right about Badger and she was wrong. I was right to trust him with the message, because I had good reason to think a conventional letter might not arrive. I meant to send a backup letter in the morning, I really did. If we hadn't found the body, I wouldn't have been captured." He waited, hoping to be dismissed.

Roland was not finished. "Before leaving here, you will write a detailed letter of apology to Grand Master."

That was too much! "Grand Master is an incompetent oaf!"

The Chancellor stiffened. "Guardsman, watch your tongue! You are speaking of the senior officer of the Order to which I also have the honor of belonging. If you refuse to apologize to him, then you will write a detailed letter to the King explaining what you just said!"

"Very well!" Wart said recklessly. He was flying now. "I'll do that. I will point out that if Grand Master had bothered to investigate Badger's erratic behavior, he would have realized it was caused by more than a normal dose of seniors' nerves. Then he would have uncovered a conspiracy that would have taken the King's life at the next binding. By removing Badger from Ironhall, I undoubtedly saved—"

"That was pure luck!"

Stalwart pulled himself back to ground level. He was the most junior Blade in the kingdom. Who was he to bad-mouth Grand Master? "True! You are quite right, my lord. It was luck."

"If you will promise to keep your opinions to

yourself," the great man said warily, "I will waive the letter of apology. His Majesty will be informed of events, of course."

"Thank you, my lord. Have I your permission to withdraw?" Stalwart began to heave his bulk off the stool, planning another trip to the kitchens.

"No. Wait a minute." Lord Roland reached out finger and thumb to snuff a guttering candle. "This affair will never be made public. The ringleaders will be tried in secret and I'm sure many will be executed in secret, too. The rest will be locked up forever. We were all very lucky that His Grace survived this conspiracy. Digby did write a letter."

"And the traitors intercepted it, Badger said."

"He wrote *two* letters. The second one he sent from Buran, on his way home. He was a Blade, after all; not quite the blockhead many people thought him." The great man looked inquiringly at Stalwart.

"Certainly." Stalwart wondered uneasily what had happened to Digby's sword. Better not to mention it.

"You will find . . . You will learn, as I have, that conspiracy is much less common in this world than plain, brainless incompetence."

"Er . . . my lord?"

"About two hours after you and Emerald left the palace, I arrived at my office to start a long day's work. I found Lord Digby's name in my appointment book. I made inquiries, of course. I learned that he had tried to see me the day he returned, the day before his death, but I was occupied with arrangements for the reception."

Was it possible that the notoriously impassive Lord Roland was actually looking a little embarrassed?

"Digby did not send his letters to Sir Snake, because he knew the King would disapprove. Having discovered an incompetent sheriff, he wrote posthaste to me. It was absolutely his duty to do that. He also mentioned a curious coincidence about the silver streak in the Prior's hair. That was enough to set my britches on fire, I can tell you!"

Wart stared blankly. "But . . .?"

"My clerks," the Chancellor said ruefully, "had treated the letter as entirely routine. It was put away for consideration at the regular meeting of the Council next month."

"Ah!" He had good reason to feel embarrassed!

"I sent a courier after you—he missed you, obviously, probably because you went around by Ironhall. Snake and the Old Blades had been chasing their tails looking for octograms until they were all exhausted. I dragged the King out of bed to appoint a new sheriff, commandeered the Yeomen Lancers, and came boiling out here to Nythia to rescue you. As it happened, you didn't really need all that much rescuing . . ."

Lord Roland broke off to glare at his listener. His fist slammed down on the desk. "I have to put up with that supercilious smirk when the King's behind it. *I don't need to take it from you!*"

"No! No, of course not, my lord!" Stalwart said hastily.

Durendal sighed. "Sometimes even the best of us have to fall back on luck—*brother.*" He smiled as if he meant it.

Young Stalwart's story begins with "Book One of the King's Daggers," but the world of the legendary knights is first introduced in

The Gilded Chain:
A Tale of the King's Blades
by Dave Duncan,
now available from Avon Eos.

As unwanted, rebellious boys, they found refuge in the grim school of Ironhall. They emerged years later as nimble and deadly young men, the finest in the realm—the King's Blades. A magical ritual of a sword through the heart bound each of them to absolute loyalty to defend his ward—if not the King himself—then whomever else he designated. And the greatest Blade of them all was Sir Durendal.

But a lifelong dream of riding to war at the side of his adored liege—of battling traitors and monsters and rising high in the court—is dashed when Durendal is bonded till death, not to his beloved King, but an effete noble fop. Yet from this inauspicious beginning, twisting destiny has many strange and inscrutable plans for the young knight, prophesied to be the mightiest hero that ever lived.

At last the great door and the snowy steps beyond—Lord Roland was about to leave Greymere for the last time, venturing out into a very unpleasant-looking winter's night. Never would his own fireside seem more welcome.

The King came and went from palace to palace: Nocare, Greymere, Wetshore, Oldmart, and others. Court was where the King was, but government was where the paper was; and the clerks and counters, lawyers and lackeys, labored year-round in the capital, Grandon. Even now, when the King had shut himself up in Falconsrest for Long Night, the pens still scratched busily in Greymere chancellery. Carriages were held ready day and night for the convenience of senior officials.

The weathered, square-faced head porter had borne the grandiose title of Gentleman Usher for longer than anyone could remember, perhaps even himself. Roland had bid him many thousands of good morrows and good evens. Now the old man looked ready to melt like the slush on the cobbles. All he could say was, "I got my orders, my lord." There was a coach and four in clear sight sheltering under the arch, awaiting his hail, but he had his orders. He probably had hopes of a small pension from the King if he continued to behave himself for the next couple of years—and did not die of misery in the next few minutes. He had his orders.

Lord Roland had never owned a coach of his own, unless one counted the one his wife used. He had rarely in his life carried money. He did not even have a horse of his own at the palace just now, but he needed to proceed home with as much dignity as possible, and a two-hour walk through the streets and out into the countryside in his chancellor's robes would not be dignified. Kromman wanted to hurt, but then Kromman had been nursing his hatred for a generation.

Quarrel's eager young face seemed dangerously inflamed under the rushlights. He was practically quivering. Roland gestured him forward and took a step back.

"Gentleman Usher," he said from behind his guardian's shoulder, "this is very embarrassing for me. My Blade, Sir Quarrel, has not been with me long enough to learn how things are done in the palace. Thus, when I sent him on ahead to order a carriage, he did not understand that the ensuing problem was not of your devising. I am sure he would not really have hurt you, but—"

Quarrel's sword hissed from its scabbard.

Gentleman Usher lost his look of despair. "Ah, noble Sir Blade! Pray be not hard on a poor old man or deprive his fourteen grandchildren of their beloved grandfather!"

"Verily!" Quarrel said. "Dost thou not summon yonder carriage full speedily and direct it to a place congruous to my ward's desires, then I shall expeditiously slit thee into elementary eighths."

"Forsooth? Hold it under my chin, lad—it'll look better. Coach! Coach!"

As Roland climbed into the carriage, he could hear Gentleman Usher directing the driver, still at sword point. When the horses began to move, Quarrel swung nimbly aboard and closed the door. The team pulled out of the palace gates, clattering into the night-filled streets.

Farewell, Greymere!

"Thank you, Sir Quarrel. That was a very nice piece of highwaymanship. And I congratulate you on your verbal feinting earlier."

"My pleasure, my lord." He did not laugh, but his smile was audible.